THE RUNNING GIRL

ALSO BY BEVAN AMBERHILL IN THIS SERIES

The Bloody Man

THE RUNNING GIRL

A Jean-Claude Keyes Mystery

by Bevan Amberhill

A *Midnight Original* MURDER MYSTERY

THE MERCURY PRESS

The publisher gratefully acknowledges the financial assistance of the Canada
Council and the Ontario Arts Council, as well as that of the Government of
Ontario through the Ontario Publishing Centre.

The author wishes to thank Emma Challis,
for her new translations of excerpts from the poetry of Catullus.

Edited by Beverley Daurio
Cover design by Scott McKowen
Composition and page design by TASK

Printed and bound in Canada by Metropole Litho
Printed on acid-free paper
First Edition
1 2 3 4 5 99 98 97 96 95

Canadian Cataloguing in Publication Data

Amberhill, Bevan
The running girl
ISBN 1-55128-019-1
I. Title
PS8551.M34R86 1995   C813'.54   C95-93232-6
PR9199.3.A73R86 1995

Represented in Canada by the Literary Press Group
Distributed by General Distribution Services

The Mercury Press
137 Birmingham Street
Stratford, Ontario
Canada   N5A 2T1

For Aurora, dancer of the dawn.
And for Jerome, Prince of Frogs.

Cui dono lepidum nouum libellum
arido modo pumice expolitum?
quare habe tibi quidquid hoc libelli
qualecumque... o patrona uirgo.
— Catullus

(To whom do I give this neat little book
all new and polished and ready to go?
Here's the book, for whatever it's worth
I want you to have it, virgin patroness.)

Prologue

For February nineteenth through the twenty-first, the weather reports predicted bearable conditions: temperatures in southwestern Ontario were to hover near zero degrees Celsius under sunny skies. Meteorological analysts on television wore smiles as they announced that Wiarton Willie's Groundhog Day forecast had been correct: winter, the experts said, was definitely retreating.

The most severe winter storms in the area often occurred during February. However, everyone happily nodded in agreement with the weatherpeople, exhibiting that selective form of amnesia concerning the cruel perversity of Canadian winters that keeps Canadians from emigrating *en masse* to Hawaii.

Beasts that burrowed (including one very embarrassed groundhog), and those that flew and dwelled in caves, however, took a very different attitude toward the immediate future. Rabbits and squirrels dug more deeply into their nests, while chickadees and wrens sought snug shelter among rocks and trees and buildings. Even the bears woke briefly and huddled back into the furthest reaches of their habitations.

Because beyond the range of satellites and the ken of prognosticating software, in the primal place where tsunami are seeded and hurricanes nurtured, gigantic hands of ice, snow, and wind were forming into fists and rising, to once again smite the innocent, upturned face of this frozen land.

1.

Jean-Claude Keyes was contemplating murder, or, more accurately, he was planning mechanicide. The victim-to-be, a malevolent presence on his desk, crouched only a few feet away, amid open books, empty mugs, tumblers, and the next-to-last draft of Keyes' current manuscript... which might have ended up being the final draft, if the computer had had its current way.

The machine in question (and in danger) was doing the microchip equivalent of grinning at its owner's impotent rage, displaying an error message that was incomprehensible to Keyes. Following a string of numbers, the cheerfully lit box onscreen announced:

```
CRITICAL FILES HAVE BECOME
IRREPARABLY CORRUPT.
SYSTEM-WIDE FAILURE IS
IMMINENT IF YOU CONTINUE.
OKAY?
```

"It is *not* okay!" Keyes growled at the device. "Why do I let people talk me into these things?" He had purchased the computer on the advice of his editor, who evidently understood the things as well as she did the arcane structures of both the English language and the Canadian publishing industry. He should instead have heeded the words of a friend, an Ojibway poet who had warned him that computers were "mean little sidewinders." But, no, Keyes had put his trust in Corinna, and after three weeks of wading through manuals, he had actually begun trying to use the monster. He had managed to enter the editorial revisions to *Vengeance: A User's Manual*, his new biography of Canadian classical Greek scholar Caitlin Harper, safely into the hard drive. The machine had then printed out the pages in Cyrillic characters. And now this.

"You will pay, Corinna Brand," Keyes said as he reached for the phone, hoping that Corinna was having a nap, or in the bath, or doing something equally pleasant which he could interrupt. He glanced at his watch. It wasn't working, either, and so it was with a disproportionate sense of relief that he discovered the telephone to be functioning almost as it should.

"Hi! You've reached the number of Corinna Brand. I can't take your call right now as I'm doing something absolutely fascinating. Please leave your name, number, the time of your call and any message, and I'll get back to you as soon as I can. 'Bye now."

Keyes prefaced his recorded plea for help with an overly dramatic sigh of frustration. He hung up wondering if it was his fate to get no work at all done this day. Another of Corinna's odd ideas was that deadlines were a good thing, and one was fast approaching for Keyes, a deadline which the computer was *supposed* to help him meet. He began to smile in the direction of the stubborn Iron Maiden on his desk. "If I miss my deadline, it's *your* fault," he announced, and felt better.

Work out of the way, he began to plan how he could most enjoyably waste his last quiet winter afternoon in his Toronto apartment. My last day *of any kind* here, he reminded himself, as he negotiated his way among boxes and cartons to part the curtains which overlooked College Street. A light snow, beginning to fall, effectively defeated the idea of a walk down to the Bar Italia for a bowl of soup; Keyes hated snowy days in the city— the pretty whiteness soon turned into grimy slush that made everyone damp and grumpy. All right then, he thought, a nice fire, a heavily caloric lunch, and some music. Satisfied with this sybaritic escape from his immediate problems, he began searching the unsealed cartons of archaic vinyl records, which, in the DAT and CD èra, were becoming either completely worthless or unimaginably valuable, depending on whom one talked to.

Keyes' collection contained only two genres of music: opera and blues. Although he was not talented musically, he liked music quite broadly and generally; he collected opera because of his background and blues because he was sometimes blue. Most of his collection had been accumulated years before the new technologies put him off this hobby altogether.

Today was definitely an opera day. There was a brooding, melancholy sky to go with the cold, and he was only fifteen hours or so away from leaving behind forever this place, which had become his sanctum, to attempt to set down roots in a new and sometimes savage land. It was a day for Wagner.

Twenty minutes later, Keyes was sitting in his deep black leather chair (tagged Handle With Care for the movers) with an expression of bliss on his worn features. *Tristan und Isolde* moaned about him at a volume just safely below the tolerance of his neighbours.

Keyes' love affair with opera had been initiated by his French mother, who was a singer. She had a fine, undertrained contralto voice which she exhibited in church choirs and amateur theatricals. Whenever there was opera to be heard in Montreal, she went to hear it, and as soon as her son was old enough to sit through long evenings of theatre, she had taken him with her.

Keyes hadn't exactly liked opera when he was young; he had imagined himself bored by it. But he never forgot those long evenings, never forgot the narcissistic pleasure of being dressed up in a jacket and tie— although he complained about both— never forgot the thrill of being his mother's escort, sitting beside her in the darkness, aware of her warm satin-clad body next to him, hearing her humming beneath the music, hearing her catch her breath at some dramatic development of plot or melody, hearing her little sighs that he did not understand...

He had thought her quite beautiful then, on those gala evenings at the opera. He thought her quite beautiful now, for that matter. Sixty-five years old, she wore her white hair loose and flowing around her shoulders, and refused to play the role of little old lady. She was, however, increasingly housebound and hampered by arthritis in her hands and neck. Keyes could not imagine her as a shut-in, confined to her small flat in Montreal, but her doctors had indicated that this was a possibility for which she should be prepared.

Keyes was an only child. He had never known his father, and knew nothing about him other than the fact that Madame Keyes had chosen not to accept the man's honourable proposal of marriage. But, she had proven to be a loving and capable mother, and Keyes had never really been troubled by the lack of a permanent male presence in their household. She had been his closest friend, his collaborator in every adventure. She had even found him his first girlfriend.

Madame Keyes had supported them by working as a seamstress, specializing in costume, for a house that supplied fancy dress to Montreal's party-makers and also, on occasion, to its theatre companies. Somewhere in her busy life she had obtained an expert knowledge of "period" dress. She was good at applying lace, braid, and sequins to coats and frocks of many epochs. She was good at painted decoration.

Among the women who worked with Madame Keyes at the costume shop was a certain Lisette, an aspiring dancer, eighteen years old, and the lover of an actor who was often on tour. Keyes was two years younger than Lisette when they were introduced to one another by his mother. Madame Keyes brought Lisette home to dinner sometimes, when the girl's actor was away; Madame Keyes sometimes kept Lisette overnight, when the weather was bad; eventually, Madame Keyes put Lisette in bed with her young son.

Keyes, after years of fantasy and masturbation, thought he had died and gone to Paradise the first night that Lisette slept with him.

His heart was broken, of course, when the actor came home.

"I know, chéri," his mother had said, consoling him, "I know."

Somehow he knew that she did.

There was a succession of lovers after Lisette, and usually they were entertainers— dancers, singers, actresses. None of them were very settled or very dependable. Keyes remained unmarried. Years after he had left home and become an actor himself, he met a wise woman who told him that only men who had been raised among women— meaning sisters— made good husbands. That was because, she explained, they were not idealistic about women. They loved, but like fond brothers; they did not adore.

Keyes had a tendency to adore.

Listening to *Tristan*, he remembered Lisette. He remembered his mother, too, as she had been when he was eleven and she thirty.

He got up, went to his cache of mid-move rations, and poured himself a small glass of red wine. He also took out a box of chocolate cream-filled delicacies that his mother had sent from Montreal.

("You are too thin, chéri," she said whenever she saw him. "Maigre...")

"To move or not to move... that *was* the question," Keyes mumbled around a mouthful of pastry. But by this time next week, he would be settled in his quaint little (*very* little) brick cottage in Stratford, where, this very day, perhaps this very moment, his lawyer was closing the deal on his new home. This was Keyes' first experience with buying a house, and he had left the details in the hands of those whose business it was to facilitate such matters. A full cast of realtors, lawyers, painters, and movers was participating in the Jean-Claude Keyes production of *Little House in Ontario*, but it was worth it— tomorrow all Keyes had to do was drive to Stratford, sign twenty or thirty pieces of paper, pick up his keys, and step onto the stage of this latest phase of his life.

Keyes had always lived in cities, but in his opinion the metropoli of the world were becoming less livable every day.

Soon he would actually be part of a community of manageable size, where he could wander the streets at three a.m. in search of a cup of coffee without fear (or without *much* fear) of being mugged or murdered or molested. He would be on a first name basis with many of the people he met on the street, and able to afford his mortgage payments...

And, if necessary, his mother could come and live with him, should the arthritis and advancing years prove stronger than she was. It was not something she expected of her son, but neither was it something her son begrudged her. They had lived separate lives for many years, but Keyes was ready to provide sanctuary for her if called upon to do so.

As for his own needs, Keyes had been finding it harder and harder to write in Toronto, now that he was doing it full time. Within the last two years, the city had grown louder and his apartment smaller.

Still, he couldn't help wondering if Stratford would be as charming and civilized as his memory had painted it, once he was a bona fide resident rather than merely a transient actor performing at the Festival, or a giddy tourist attending its plays. At least he knew Stratford would be *calmer* than it had been on his last visit– which had been more Grand Guignol than Shakespearean, because of the murder of Alan Wales.

Keyes had never really quite sorted out how that brief and intense immersion in death and betrayal had affected him. He liked to think that he was a gentler, more responsible man because of it all. But then, he also liked to think that he was Humphrey Bogart...

He frowned slightly. An alien instrument was making itself known in the middle of the grand, sprawling extravagance of Richard Wagner's music; it took several seconds for him to recognize this noise as the ringing of his telephone. With some regret, he set aside his small pleasures and lurched to his feet, having no answering machine to deal with the intrusion.

"Hello!" he bellowed over the Liebestraum.

Corinna's ever-cheerful voice sounded in Keyes' right ear.

"Claude? Corinna. What is that godawful racket? Sounds like tin elephants mating in an ironworks!"

"It's Wagner," Keyes replied primly. "Hold on, I'll turn it down."

"Please!" Corinna's voice begged as he leaned over to adjust the volume. "Oh, that's much better. Your message said you were having problems with Daphne."

Keyes took a deep breath, swallowing a hypocritical lecture on the evils of anthropomorphism.

"That damned machine does not have a name! And if it did, it would certainly not be Daphne!" He then explained in as much detail as possible the computer's malfeasance.

"Oh, that's no problem, Claude," Corinna said when he finished. "Just boot it up again."

"I intend to," he said. "Where is its ass?"

"My grandmother's name was Daphne, so don't you dare kick her, Jean-Claude Keyes!"

Keyes privately admitted defeat with a grin, and pressed the RESET button. When he returned his attention to the telephone, Corinna had ceased gloating over her logic-chopping.

"Listen, Claude, since this is your last night in Babylon, Sam and I want to take you out to a new club that's having its gala opening tonight; I know you've been working hard on the final revisions and your packing. What about a night out?"

Keyes considered his options as the computer screen went through the complicated dance of re-arranging its electrons or ions or croutons or whatever the hell it used.

"Sure, why not?"

"Great! It's called The Rhinestone Cow, and it's right beside that Malaysian restaurant on Queen Street that we went to once, remember? I'll meet you there nine-ish. Sam says there's no cover charge and it doesn't get busy until eleven or so. And bundle up— I just listened to the weather, and it sounds like welders are going to be doing a brisk trade in brass monkeys by tonight. 'Bye. Give my love to Daphne."

Sometimes, Keyes thought as he hung up, that woman is mystical in her ability to sense the needs and desires of her authors. He could not remember when he had last been out socially of an evening, and, if he stayed in, he would only brood about the wisdom of his decision to leave Toronto after so many years of making the place work for him, if only marginally...

Later, as he was mulling over what a man might possibly wear to a place with the curious name of The Rhinestone Cow, Keyes realized that he had a more immediate and less existential problem than that of his relocation: he was going out that night, and his clothing was already stowed away for shipping.

2.

Keyes opened and re-taped several boxes before he found his favourite outfit: an army-surplus greatcoat over battered brown leather jacket, battered grey turtleneck sweater, and battered blue Levi's, supplemented by the winter necessities of woolen scarf and gloves.

"I wish I had a hat," he muttered at the mirror. He had never quite found the perfect hat for his head size and temperament, and so wore none at all, which was foolish of him. He lived in a city that was frequently chilly.

As Corinna had forewarned, it was freezing cold in the street when he went down to meet the cab he had called.

"Where to?" the driver asked him. He was a young man, brown-skinned and raven-haired— Indian or Pakistani or Persian, Keyes guessed. He glanced at the identification tag above the driver's head. The dark man's name was Bert Christensen.

A Swede? Keyes asked himself, looking again at the brown

skin and the ravenish hair. He shrugged and leaned forward to give his destination.

"Where, sir?"

Evidently the driver was new to his job, perhaps new to Toronto.

"It's on Queen, just past Havelock."

"Hav-a-lot? I don't know Hav-a-lot, sir."

"All right... How well do you know College Street?"

"College Street? No, sir, I don't know College Street."

"We're on College Street," Keyes said gently. "Do you know which way is west?"

Christensen thought for a moment. "West? That's a difficulty, sir. No, sir, I don't know west."

"Okay, never mind. How are you on right and left?"

Christensen giggled and raised his left hand. "This is left, sir."

"There you go. Straight ahead, then. I'll tell you when it's time to turn left."

Christensen let out the clutch abruptly; the cab leapt ahead and flung itself into the westward flowing traffic.

"Very good, sir. Very good."

A little while later, to Keyes' surprise, he descended safely from the taxi directly in front of the Malaysian restaurant Corinna had cited as landmark. He gave a bill to Christensen, then glanced at the meter. It had never been turned on.

"Keep the change," Keyes said.

"Thank you, sir," the driver said. Once again the clutch was released with a jolt and the cab roared away, still on a westward bearing.

I wonder where he'll end up? Keyes mused as the cab

disappeared in the iron torrent of traffic. Thunder Bay, Medicine Hat, Buffalo Jump...?

A façade had recently been applied to the structure next to the restaurant, a three storey building that had probably once been a store with flats above. A large rectangular sign of brightly blinking lights identified it as The Rhinestone Cow. Keyes shook his head, perplexed all over again by the name. Planking and paint made the building look as if it belonged to the old West, to Tombstone or Dodge City or Waco, or to the replicas of them built on the movie lots of Southern California. I'm a long way from California, Keyes thought, as a sharp gust of wind blew snow into his face. He shivered and hurried for the entrance.

As soon as he pushed open the door, Keyes heard the music of steel guitars and fiddles, and a snatch of lyrics:

My nose's been red and my heart has been blue,
From drinkin' and thinkin' what I'll do without you.

Two very big doormen stood just inside the entrance. They were dressed in cowboy costumes, but of the singing movie cowboy variety, gaudy with rhinestones and outrageous colours. They were so tall and broad they seemed to be supporting the ceiling.

Like atlantids, Keyes thought in some neo-classical corner of his brain, active of late no doubt because of his inquiries into the life of a Euripides scholar. The cowhands looked Keyes over carefully, but he passed between them unchallenged and as calmly as he might have passed between statues at the baroque portal of a palace in Prague or Vienna.

"G'd evening, friends," he murmured as he went.

"Yo," said one of the giants.

"Hi," said the other.

Already the eyes of the atlantids were on the door that was closing behind Keyes.

The Rhinestone Cow's lobby was outfitted to look like a country store with rough-hewn posts and lintels, wooden barrels, and rude pine shelving. The wares for sale in the store were a mixture of haberdashery and tack. There were many flamboyant western-style shirts, hats, britches, boots. There was lots of leather, including whips for all purposes: riding crops, buggy whips, dressage whips, bullwhips, and whips for occasions that Keyes could not imagine.

All this treasure was presided over by a slender, platinum-haired cowboy wearing a shirt decorated with red and white embroidered roses. His jeans were too tight, surely, to allow him to mount a horse. His boots were marvels of sculpted cowhide. There was a large silver star pinned to the chest of his shirt, with, Keyes assumed, his name on it. Keyes had trouble reading the star because the handwriting was so bad, but it was either "Tex" or "Sex." Tex, I hope, Keyes thought.

"Anything I can help you with?" Tex asked sweetly as Keyes headed for the stairs.

Keyes paused. "As a matter of fact, I would sort of like a hat..."

"We have lots," the blonde cowboy said, waving toward a corner where hats rose in clusters like hollyhocks in a rustic garden.

Tempted, Keyes gazed on these headpieces for a moment, then shook his head.

"I'd better find my date first," he said. "Maybe later."

"Any time," Tex or Sex said. "Whenever."

Keyes climbed to the second floor, passing through swinging saloon doors to the site of the action. There was a long, old-style bar and a dance floor, the boundaries of which resembled hitching posts. On a stage beyond was a six-piece band: piano, bass, fiddle, drums, guitar, and steel guitar. The boys in the band were playing "The Tennessee Waltz."

The bar was crowded with cowboys drinking beer, the dance floor with cowboys dancing with other cowboys, and occasionally cowgirls dancing with cowgirls. Keyes did not see Corinna anywhere, so he went to the bar. The bartender was a brawny cowhand with short hair greased straight back, and several tattoos.

"What'll it be, mister?" Keyes was asked in a gentle soprano voice at odds with the rest of the image.

"A beer, I guess. Say, I'm looking for a woman— five-six, or seven, brown hair, talks a lot..." Keyes made vague gestures to suggest Corinna's figure.

"Lots of luck," the bartender said. "Did you say light beer?"

"No," Keyes said almost aggressively. "Ale."

The bartender grinned. "Whatever you say, pardner."

"I was wondering about the name of this place," Keyes said when the bartender returned with his beer. "What exactly is a Rhinestone Cow?"

The bartender's eyebrows arched in exasperation. "I've been explaining this all night! That is *not* our name. The contractor who did the sign got the instructions and specifications all wrong, and no one noticed until the sign was in place! *This* is the real name!"

The bartender pointed to a coaster beside Keyes' hand. "The Rhinestone Cowperson," it read.

"Oh," Keyes said. "Thanks."

"There you are!" shrilled a voice behind Keyes.

He turned. Corinna stood before him. She was almost unrecognizable in her western drag. Keyes knew only her young executive persona: expensive pin-striped suits, lots of cashmere, serious shoes, serious briefcases. Even when they had been out together socially before she had had a corporate look about her.

"Hey," Keyes said, "you look so much like a cowboy I couldn't find you in the crowd."

"You should have checked my brand."

"The Brand brand?"

"Oh, Claude!" she grimaced. "You remember Sam, don't you?"

Keyes did.

"Hello, Sam," he said holding out his hand.

Sam shook the hand. "Hello, Claude. Do you waltz?"

"Mostly I just watch," Keyes said, as his beer was set on the bar. "I'll run a tab," he told the bartender, who nodded. It would take quite a number of beers, Keyes reflected, to get to the point where he could waltz.

"*I* still waltz," Corinna said. "Do you mind, Claude?"

Keyes shook his head. "Not at all. You kids go ahead and have a good time."

They did. Together Corinna and Sam skipped away and joined the promenade of waltzers who moved in a slow and stately oval motion around the dance floor. Because of the western costume that everyone wore— everyone but Keyes— it was quite a spectacle. There was an astonishing variety of hats on display: tall hats and hats of low crown, black hats, grey hats, brown hats, hats with feathers, with silver conches, hats with leather bands. The shirts were as various, and the boots even more so.

Everyone was having a fine time. There was a lot of laughter, good-tempered, spontaneous.

Must be the light beer, Keyes thought, as he sipped at his heavy, masculine ale.

The two men on his right at the bar were talking about marketing schemes; the two on his left were talking about Key West.

"You ready, pal?" the bartender asked, amiably.

Keyes nodded. "Make it a light one this time."

The waltz was a long medley of waltzes, and Corinna danced on and on with Sam. She was leading, which didn't surprise Keyes. She always led, no matter which of life's dances she was involved in or what the figure of the dance. When the medley was finished Sam and Corinna danced a two-step, or a number of them. Always the movement on the floor was large and flowing like a great, slow, counter-clockwise whirlpool.

Keyes almost felt like dancing himself, but dancing was something he had decided years before that he hadn't time or inclination for. The long-departed Lisette had danced, often and well; she had danced her way back to her actor...

"Too bad, Claude," Corinna said breathlessly at his elbow, as she and Sam took a brief pause at the watering hole.

"What's too bad?"

"That you don't dance. Ready, Sam?"

Both downed their drinks, then joined the widening gyre of a Virginia reel. Keyes had never seen Corinna have so much fun. In fact he had never seen her have fun at all. She was always too busy with shop talk and deals. He was relieved that tonight she seemed to have checked that side of herself at the door. Keyes talked shop only when he had to, and he talked deals only when he could see starvation looming in his future.

"Excuse me," said a voice over Keyes' right shoulder, a pleasantly modulated male voice with the precise syllabic pronunciation which Keyes associated with the theatre. Keyes turned, readying a small speech which he had carefully prepared as soon as he had recognized the nature of the Rhinestone's clientele— a polite statement of his unrepentant heterosexuality.

The stranger must have seen this in Keyes' face, or in his body language; he held up both of his hands, palms out toward Keyes, and smiled.

"Don't worry, Mr. Keyes, I'm not trying to pick you up... I'm just a fan."

Keyes saw a tall man, who, like himself, eschewed cowboy gear. He did, however, bear a strong resemblance to county singer Waylon Jennings, but with better hair and wardrobe. The stranger wore a well-cut three-piece suit of powder blue, a black silk shirt, and black, highly polished Oxfords. He also sported aviator-style spectacles, dark tinted. Keyes could not see his eyes.

"Have we met?" Keyes asked.

"No, but I've read *Cakes and Ale*— I recognized you from the dust-jacket photo..."

"So you're the one!" Keyes laughed, not without a certain melancholy. The book referred to was Keyes' biography of Stratford Festival acting veteran Seamus O'Reilly. *Cakes and Ale* had sold a few hundred copies to Canada's theatre community, but now Keyes feared it was destined for the remainder bins at Wal-Mart. Money, fame, and glowing reviews had not been among his principal reasons for writing Seamus' biography, but still...

Keyes returned his attention to the stranger, who had bought him a beer.

"Thanks," Keyes said, raising the bottle to his benefactor.

"No, I should be thanking *you*, Mr. Keyes," the stranger said. "I love the theatre, and I've followed Seamus O'Reilly's career from its very beginning. I have no artistic talent myself, only the gift of making money, but I believe it's important that those *with* talent should be recognized. Books like yours... it's hard to put into words. For me it is, anyway..."

The stranger's voice trailed off, but Keyes heard a faint echo of something like loneliness or regret. Keyes thought of how he himself had occasionally wished for facility in making money rather than paragraphs, and shook his head slightly at the grim humour of whoever or whatever passed out skills and abilities at birth.

"Anyway," the stranger continued, "I won't intrude on you any longer. I just wanted to say hello, to say thank you, and to shake your hand."

Keyes took the offered hand, which had a very expensive-looking ring on it. Then the tall stranger turned and picked his way through the spinning dancers toward the exit.

"How about that?" Keyes said aloud. "Who *was* that man?"

"I don't know," said the bartender, who had been polishing glasses nearby, "but it looks like he left you something."

There was a small paper bag on the bar. Keyes' name and a short note were written on it in delicate calligraphy. "To help you continue your work," it said. There was no signature.

Inside was a small, voice-activated cassette recorder of the type currently popular among writers of all disciplines. Its aluminum casing flashed briefly silver as Keyes examined it under the bar lights.

"Oh, God, another gadget," commented the Luddite in Keyes' soul, but in a deeper part of that soul was a pleasant, warm glow. He slipped the device into the inner pocket of his jacket, where it settled gently over his heart.

Corinna and Sam danced for another two hours, then the

music stopped and a man came onstage who introduced himself as "Chuck, the Rhinestone manager." He thanked everyone for coming, then began to distribute gifts to the evening's best dancers. It was something like a rodeo Keyes had once attended in Calgary, except that the prizes here were for waltz, two-step, and polka, instead of barrel-racing, pole-bending, and cattle-cutting. There were also prizes for costume: Best Boots, Best Britches, Best Hat... The prizes were mostly articles of clothing or tack from the shop downstairs.

Corinna and Sam joined him at the bar.

"Did you see, Claude?" Corinna bubbled. "We won an award."

She held up a glittering object.

"And it is...?"

"A rhinestone horseshoe. We got it for being the most original couple."

"Original? What does that mean?"

Sam helped out. "I suspect it means we were the only couple of mixed gender on the floor."

"I don't care why we won it! It's ours," Corinna said positively.

"Why don't you keep it, C.B.?" Sam suggested. "It won't go with the decor of my apartment."

"I'd love to... but I sure can't dance with it— it's heavy. Hang on to it for me, Claude."

Keyes took the shiny thing and said he would take good care of it. The Most Original Couple melted back into the throng of dancers.

Half an hour later they reappeared.

"That's it, Sam," Corinna said wearily but happily. "I've got an early and long day tomorrow."

"But *tonight* is barely pubescent!" Sam the Indefatigable complained.

"Now, don't think it wasn't lovely, because it was, but you go dance with someone else."

Sam glanced about the room.

"I suppose there must be *some*one here I know."

"Cut it out, Sam," Corinna said, laughing. "You know half the guys here, and many of them in the Biblical sense."

Sam smiled sadly. He was a handsome man, Keyes thought, closer to fifty than to forty, but so fit and well-cared for that he looked thirty-five.

"Those were the days," Sam said, "but no more... no more. Now I only dance." He turned to Keyes. "Nice seeing you, Claude. You'll escort C.B. home?"

Keyes promised that he would. Sam moved away. His hat, a white one, was soon lost among the others.

"Finish your beer," Corinna commanded. "I'm sleepy."

"I don't need to finish it, but I should pay for it."

He summoned the bartender and settled his tab.

"Thanks, pard. Drop in again when you're out this way," the bartender said.

Sam danced by with someone new.

"That's Jules," Corinna explained to Keyes. "He does dogs."

"The hell you say!"

"I *mean* he's a hairdresser, for dogs. He runs the most elegant dog-bathing shop in town. He does tinting, streaking, tipping..."

Keyes remembered that an inordinate number of dog motifs were often in evidence in Sam's book-cover designs. "I guess he and Sam have a lot to talk about."

"They do, as a matter of fact."

Keyes could see that this was true, as he watched Sam and Jules two-stepping gracefully round the dance floor. Sam was an excellent dancer, Keyes had already noticed, far better than Corinna. Jules, as Corinna had been, was leading. He, too, was far better than she. Together the two danced wonderfully well.

"I hope you weren't bored," Corinna said as they went down the stairs.

"Why would I be bored? There was a lot to watch... all those hats."

"You should have a hat."

"I was thinking that as I came in," Keyes said.

The shop on the ground floor was closed, however, so Keyes went on hatless, as usual.

"Adios, amigos," he said as they passed the atlantids.

"Yo," said one.

"'Bye," said the other.

"Where's the cab?" Corinna asked, shivering, as if she expected one to be waiting for her, or as if she expected Keyes to have arranged for one to be waiting.

"I don't see one at the moment."

What Keyes did see was three large men stumbling along the sidewalk toward them. They wore big-toed unlaced work boots, blue jeans sagging under ample bellies, plaid jackets, and baseball caps. All three appeared drunk.

"You girls have a good time in there?" the biggest of the three said, gesturing toward the door to the nightclub.

Keyes continued to look for a taxi. He was more interested in getting out of the cold than in exchanging pleasantries with rednecks.

"Bugger off!" Corinna spat at the big man.

Keyes looked at her in dismay.

"What'd you say, bitch?" the man said, closing the distance between them.

"Take it easy, Corinna," Keyes murmured.

Only then did Keyes realize that Corinna was as drunk as the man she had yelled at. Perhaps it wasn't light beer she'd been drinking in the dance hall, or maybe she had been drinking before the evening started. That, he reflected, would not be unlike her.

"I said bugger off, asshole!"

Keyes groaned, then something about the asshole's cap caught his attention— it was his evening for noticing hats. It wasn't a baseball cap after all, but a beer store cap. Although it was shaped like a baseball cap, it advertised Coors beer, not the Blue Jays. Keyes glanced quickly at the other two men. Their caps proclaimed Miller and Bud.

Keyes was not an advocate of Free Trade. He had a terrible hunch that anything the American government wanted so desperately was likely to benefit the American government far more than anyone else. Coors, Miller, and Bud were examples of Free Trade, he considered: inferior beers which found favour with inferior Canadians... at least judging from these three.

These ruminations occurred in an instant, and during that instant Coors plodded to within arm's length— his own arm's— of Keyes and Corinna.

"So who's gonna make me, bitch?" Coors said. "You? Or maybe your fag boyfriend?"

Keyes did not take offence easily, nor did he act in haste on those occasions when he was offended. Corinna, especially Corinna drunk, was not so diplomatic.

"Asshole!" she shrieked. Then she swung her arm and the

fist at the end of it. The blow caught Coors on the chest. He laughed and shoved his attacker. She went over backwards, sitting down hard in the fresh snow. She was winded and astonished, as if she had never been knocked down before, which was probably the case despite her constant exercizing of assertiveness techniques.

"What do you say, fag?" Coors growled. "You want some, too?"

Keyes looked solemnly at the beefy, beer-reddened face, at the ferocious, beer-reddened eyes. Then he watched as Coors' heavy right fist pulled ominously back in preparation for a punch considerably more damaging than the shove that had landed Corinna in the snow.

"What do I say?" Keyes asked whimsically. "Well... I say that's no way to treat an editor."

From her ringside seat on the sidewalk, the editor of the moment saw what happened next, but understood nothing of what she saw. What she did understand was the way the hefty Coors doubled up, dropped to his knees, rolled to his side and lay bellowing in the slushy gutter.

The door to The Rhinestone Cowperson flew open and the two atlantids appeared. They strode toward Miller and Bud, who were bending over Coors, scratching their heads in beery confusion.

"Yo!" said one of the atlantids.

"What's going on?" asked his partner.

Miller and Bud glanced at these colossi, then bolted, leaving Coors writhing and howling on the sidewalk.

The doormen looked at Keyes, who was helping Corinna to her feet.

"It's getting icy," he said blandly. "Dangerous."

A taxi prowled down the street toward them. Keyes raised his arm in a hail.

"I think he's hurt himself," Keyes said, nodding at Coors. "Maybe you should get him a cab, too."

"Or an ambulance," one of the bouncers said.

"Or an ambulance," Keyes agreed as he and Corinna climbed into the cab.

"Take it easy," Keyes warned the cab driver, a woman with a disposition as soft as sidewalks, after giving her Corinna's address. "It's getting slippery."

"Really?" the driver replied with weary irony. She did, however, drive slowly and, for a city hack, carefully.

Keyes turned his attention back to Corinna.

"You're all right, aren't you?"

She nodded. "Angry, but all right. Sore bum..."

"I'm not surprised— you went down pretty hard."

"Not as hard as that... that dickhead! What did you do to him?"

"Hit him."

"I didn't *see* you hit him."

"Fortunately, he didn't either... anyway, he was out of shape— lots of belly fat, but not much gristle. You shouldn't go street-fighting unless you're in better shape than that."

"Will he be all right? Was he badly hurt?"

"What do you care? He knocked you down."

"I don't believe in violence."

"Neither do I."

Corinna was silent for a moment.

"Where did you learn to do that?"

"What?"

"You know— fight. I don't exactly think of you as a street-fighter, Claude."

Keyes shrugged. "Oh, I've been in lots of fights. You forget I was an actor. I carried spears in a lot of shows; I was trained with long sword, short sword, rapier and foil, as well as poleaxe, halberd, partisan, quarter staff—" He struck a pose, raising Corinna's sparkling dance trophy over his head like a medieval warrior's mace. "— and rhinestone horseshoe... well, maybe not one of those exactly, but we were taught to improvise, so I improvised."

"You certainly did," Corinna laughed.

"And I was lucky— he was drunk, out of shape, and stupid, so I had an edge," Keyes said.

"But... will he be all right?"

"A hernia isn't that hard to mend these days..."

Corinna shuddered. "I still don't like it."

"Neither do I," Keyes sighed.

Despite the lateness of the hour, Keyes' telephone was ringing when he entered his apartment.

"Hello," he said, out of breath from scrabbling over cartons in the semi-darkness.

"Claude? Marcia— sorry about the time, but I've been trying to reach you all night."

"I was out watching people dance," Keyes explained. Marcia Delaney was the Stratford lawyer who was handling the house purchase for him.

"Oh, how voyeuristic of you! Listen, we've hit a last minute snag. I'm pretty sure I can sort it out tomorrow morning, but I thought I should let you know..."

"I'm listening," Keyes said, bracing himself for the type of horror story he had often heard from friends who owned their own homes. Marcia did not disappoint him.

"Well... the people in the house next door— the big yellow brick one on the corner— are claiming that because of some screw-up years ago in the surveying, your driveway is actually on *their* property."

"The neighbours own my driveway?!"

"So they think. I'm meeting with their lawyer first thing tomorrow to go over all of the plans and relevant documentation."

"And no one ever noticed this before?" Keyes asked, incredulous.

"I'm almost certain it was their attorney who did the noticing. I've locked lawsuits with this guy before— he's a sneaky little weasel who should've been disbarred and castrated a long time ago!"

"That's very encouraging, Marcia. So, has this... weasel convinced my neighbours that they need a second driveway?"

"No, that they need ten thousand dollars; that's what they want from you for that strip of land, Claude."

"Oh— and are they generously including the garage in that price?"

"No, your garage isn't in dispute, it's yours— you just can't get to it."

Keyes sighed heavily.

"Marcia, I haven't *got* ten thousand dollars— I've got barely enough to live on until my spring royalties, and I need *that* to pay you!"

Marcia made reassuring noises.

"I know, I know. Look, Claude, there's something funny about this, I'm sure of it, but I can't tell you any more until after tomorrow's meeting. Like I said, I just thought you should be aware of the situation."

"I appreciate it. Marcia... do you think I should postpone the move?"

"Do you?"

Keyes thought for a moment.

"I certainly don't want to, for several reasons. I've already paid out a lot of non-refundable cash, and the new tenants are moving into this place in two days..."

"Call me as soon as you get into Stratford. Sorry, Claude."

"That's all right. Good luck with it. I'll talk to you tomorrow some time."

"Goodnight, Claude."

"Goodnight, Marcia."

Keyes hung up the receiver. Between worrying about the news from Marcia and the sound of the rising wind outside, he did not sleep particularly well on his last night in the city of Toronto.

3.

In his dream, Keyes was living in a sub-aquatic cavern, a place lit in blues and greens, and shimmering with bubbles, fish scales, pearls and mothers of pearls. There were people about, girls and women with long, silvery hair. They were singing, or moaning, or both. In the distance he could hear a horse's hoofbeats: ditty-dum, ditty-dum, ditty dum-dum-dum-dum, dum-dum-dum-

dum... Then somebody started with a hammer; iron clanged against iron... and clanged... and clanged...

He groaned, then rolled naked and chilly out of his bed. He was no longer in a cavern beneath the Rhine; he no longer heard Alberic forging gold, or Silver galloping through the middle distance. He was in his apartment, and the telephone was ringing.

He grabbed the noisy brute from its hook.

"Claude!"

There was no mistaking the forthrightness of that voice.

"Good morning, Corinna. What time is it?"

"How should I know? Look at your watch."

Keyes looked. His watch was still broken. He had a cardboard box, carefully packed for moving, full of broken watches, one-eyed sunglasses, lockless keys, desiccated ballpoint pens, and other things of malfunction that for some reason he could not bring himself to throw out.

"What's on your mind?" Keyes asked sleepily. "Do you want to go out and bash some more fag-bashers? or maybe we could find some skinheads to pick on, or some Mounties—"

"Funny." Her voice was flat and utterly mirthless. "Listen, I'm hitching a ride to Stratford with you."

"I don't pick up hitchhikers without a very good reason," Keyes said. "Look, I'm going to live there, but why on earth do *you* have to go to Stratford?"

"Doesn't matter right now. I've got to go is all, and you've got to take me."

"What's wrong with your car?"

"I don't have a driver's license. I mean, I have one, but it's expired."

"Well," Keyes said, as reasonably as possible for a man who had had no breakfast, not even coffee, "I'm not at all sure I'm going to drive down today after all. It's snowing..."

He drew back the drapery at his window and found that it was indeed snowing with a determination which promised greater things to come.

"Only a little," Corinna said. "I just heard the weather report. The storm is going to pass way north of here. The warnings are for Sudbury, Peterborough, Ottawa—"

"Corinna..."

"Be a pal for once. Pick me up at my place. I'll be ready when you get here."

Then there was a dial tone, and Keyes felt, quite unreasonably, that some oneiric clock had started to run, and would go on running until Corinna got into his car.

"She did it again. What is wrong with my head?" he asked himself quite seriously.

4.

The girl walked rapidly, as if she might at any moment break into a run, even though the streets were newly paved with misshapen panes of slick and treacherous ice. The cold anemic February light made the girl's slight form seem even less substantial than it was.

A rucksack was slung over the girl's right shoulder. It was black, as were her clothes: black pea-jacket over black turtleneck jersey, black doeskin gloves, black jeans, soft black boots with a vaguely medieval look about them.

The wind was blowing harshly and gustily from the worst quarter, the northwest. Cold as it was, the girl wore nothing on her head. Long, fair hair whipped and coiled and streamed about her face, hiding her features, then revealing them. They were the features of a pretty, frightened child.

"Don't run," she said to herself between clenched teeth. "There's nobody after you. You don't need to run."

She came to the end of the mean street she had been following and turned left onto Railroad Avenue. Via Rail no longer served Cornerpost, Ontario, but the street name had not been changed. Nor had the train station, except that its doors and windows had been boarded up.

There was a bus stop at the railroad station now, which made no particular sense except that the building provided shelter under its broad eaves for bus travellers. There weren't many of them in Cornerpost, and the few who did travel by bus usually did so out of necessity— old people, blind people, lame people— because they couldn't drive a car or couldn't afford to own one.

Two motor coaches stopped at Cornerpost each day. One went west to London, the other east to Kitchener, which had been renamed from Berlin in 1914, as if to summarize the region's history since 1850, which was about equally shared between British settlers and those of Germanic origin.

It was toward this bus stop that the blonde girl in the black costume was urgently hurrying. She had seen no one since she left her home, at least no one on foot. Railroad Avenue was deserted. Cornerpost had become a ghost town in recent years. Once, it had been a thriving hamlet, a trading place for the farmers of the township, but bank foreclosures and farm losses had deprived the town of its reason for being. Many people had left. Those who remained had little money for shopping, or building, or maintaining— and little reason to be out in the wintery streets.

The only person likely to be out at this hour was someone

who meant to leave Cornerpost on the next bus. This was exactly the intention of the girl in black.

She pressed on, butting stubbornly into the vicious wind. She could see the station now. It was only a couple of hundred yards away, not far for someone as young as she and as eager to escape.

She was beginning to feel that she was going to make it, that she was about to be free, when she heard a sound behind her, something other than the wind. It was the grumble of an automobile engine. She hesitated and glanced over her shoulder.

The car entering Railroad Avenue behind her was a station wagon of Detroit manufacture— broad, heavy, beige, big enough to haul a largish number of children and pets and golf bags and ice skates and skis. It had about it the look of obesity which has so often been the hallmark of American automotive design. The grillework on the station wagon was monumental, but damaged on one side and rusting.

"It's him!" the girl said under her breath. Without another word or thought she began to run. The ice was treacherous. Several times she stumbled, slipped, almost fell.

The station wagon sped up, too. Quickly it overtook the running girl and pulled ahead of her, splashing her with salty slush from the gutter as it passed. Just short of the railway station it slowed and stopped. The driver's door opened and a man got out. He moved around the car to the sidewalk.

Burgess Cassell had a face that looked as if it had been recently dusted with flour. His eyes were small, red-rimmed, and deep-set. He had a ginger moustache and ginger hair that was greying at the temples where it was visible beneath his tweed cap. He wore a tan duffle coat and a muffler decorated with broad stripes in dark blue and maroon, presumably to identify him as a graduate of some university or other. More tweed was apparent in the trouser legs visible below the duffle coat. His stout oxfords were protected by low-cut black rubbers. Clearly it was his intention to look British and academic: he succeeded in looking colonial and sleazy.

The girl slowed down but kept on, marching with military determination. She looked past Cassell, then through him as he moved to block her way.

"I'm not going to let you do this, Jennet," Cassell said. "I'm not going to let you ruin your life."

The girl had no alternative but to stop. Cassell was a foot taller than she and twice her weight.

"Get out of my way!"

Cassell put out his hand. The girl shrank away from the plump paw, as floury white as the man's face.

"It's my duty to intervene..." Cassell began.

"I'm not coming back!"

"I'm afraid you have no choice."

"Yes, I do— I'm sixteen now... Get out of my way!"

"I'll do nothing of the sort. I need you, Jennet."

"Leave me alone, you freak!"

Cassell snorted something filthy, then his hand reached forward, slowly, until its fingers brushed at the girl's long hair. She gasped and backed away from his touch.

"You shouldn't talk to me that way..." Cassell stammered.

He moved toward her again, now with both arms stretched wide, to embrace her. Jennet's face contorted with loathing, but she said nothing, made no sound. Cassell bent forwards over her, as if to kiss her.

Jennet twisted away from him again, but he grabbed her arm.

His feet went out from under him and both of them fell heavily to the icy pavement.

Cassell grunted, the wind knocked out of him. Involuntarily his fingers straightened, his grip relaxed. The girl rolled away and bolted toward the bus stop.

"Jennet!" Cassell shouted after her. "I didn't mean anything...!"

He started to run after her. He didn't have Jennet's filly speed, of course, but he came on, heavily, laboriously. His white face reddened with the effort. He knew he had no hope of catching her, if she chose to go on running. Then he realized that it didn't matter. All he had to do was keep her from getting on the bus, then reason with her. Confident in his thought, he slowed down and proceeded toward the station at a more dignified pace, the pace of a pompous sergeant-major on parade.

Jennet scrambled up the steps to the station platform, then dashed down its length to the sign where the bus was supposed to halt. She looked back and saw Cassell's heavy form climbing the steps behind her. She grasped the iron post on which the sign was mounted and, like a desperate passenger on a foundering ship, held on.

At the far end of Railroad Avenue the high blunt nose of a motor coach appeared. Cassell heard it but he paid no attention. As he closed on the girl, a smug little smile decorated his doughy face.

Abruptly, the smile vanished. Another figure stepped onto the platform near the bus stop. Cassell stared and stopped. The intruder, as Cassell considered the newcomer, was a man. Obviously he had been there all along, sheltering from the raw wind by standing in a niche that once had been the station's principal doorway. The man was wearing a long, dark coat, a cowboy-style Stetson hat, and a black knotted neckerchief. He had a black valise in one hand and a musical instrument case in the other, a guitar or something of the sort.

Cassell stopped and looked at the man. He was not from Cornerpost. Cassell had never seen him before.

Less sure of himself now, Cassell started to walk again. As he got closer, he saw Jennet speak to the man, then point down the platform. The man with the musical instrument turned and peered at Cassell. Some odd trick of the wan winter light made his eyes glint red one moment and gold the next.

The stranger's face was rough and rawboned, with a jutting, grizzled chin badly in need of a shave. A hand-rolled cigarette, unlit, hung precariously between thin lips. To Burgess Cassell, the man looked rumpled and shabby and battered, not to mention obviously poor, or he wouldn't be taking a bus. He was, in fact, a compendium of many of the things that Cassell most despised.

"Hillbilly," Cassell told himself. Once again he stopped. "An alcoholic or a junky... probably dangerous."

The bus pulled up beside the platform. Air brakes hissed; the double doors opened. Scowling, Cassell watched as Jennet skipped up the steep steps into the vehicle's dark interior. The stranger glanced Cassell's way again, then followed the girl.

Cassell scowled as the coach moved away down Railroad Avenue, on its way toward a greater world, or, at the very least, towards the theatre town of Stratford, Ontario.

5.

The white Brisbane sedan, propelled by a two hundred horse-power, thirty-two valve, eight cylinder engine, guided by power-assisted rack and pinion steering with tilt and telescoping steering column, protected by dual air-bags and side impact systems, was advancing along the country highway at the dazzling speed of twenty-three miles per hour. Its eight-speaker, eighty watt stereo cassette with CD capability was silent, as were, for the moment, the four occupants of the car.

Fred Baker, George Cook, and their wives, Darlene and Earlene, were not enjoying their vacation.

Finally, Fred, who was in the driver's seat, spoke.

"Can't see bugger all, George."

George, in the passenger seat, was sympathetic.

"Me neither, Fred. Don't the windshield wipers go any faster than that?"

"They go great as a rule..."

"Snow's too heavy, I guess."

Darlene and Earlene sat in the back seat of the sedan.

"'For want of a nail,'" Darlene quoted, "'the shoe was lost. For want of a shoe, the horse was lost. For want of a horse, the battle was lost...'"

"Jesus, Darlene," George said. Darlene was George's wife.

"The question is," Earlene put in, "are we lost?"

"Do you mind, Earlene?" Fred said. Earlene was Fred's wife.

"Anyway, we're not lost," George said, cheerily rattling the road map spread across his knees. "I know exactly where we are."

"Oh, George, give us a break," Darlene said, not without a

hint of scorn in her voice. "You've never known exactly where you were in your whole life."

George turned to glare over the back of his seat. "What's that supposed to mean?"

"Now, now," Earlene purred in an attempt to keep the peace. The battles between George and Darlene Cook were legendary in Bayview, Ontario. Bayview was the retirement community in which the Bakers and Cooks had settled after Fred sold his car dealership and George had finished his forty years at Algonquin Paper Products.

"Now, now," Earlene repeated.

"Well, I'd like to know," Darlene insisted. "Where are we, George? Or where do you *think* we are?"

"I *know* where we are, damn it!"

The map rattled ominously.

"We're on County Road 17, approaching the junction with County Road 4 at West Dildo."

"Where?" Fred asked uncertainly.

"Let's see, at this speed, or lack of speed, it's hard to say exactly *where* on Road 17–"

"You see!" Darlene interrupted triumphantly.

"– exactly where on Road 17," George continued between clenched teeth, "but we've just passed Strachey, and the junction is eight... eight..."

"Miles or kilometres?" Fred asked. Serious worry shaded his voice now.

George was shaken somewhat.

"This is an old map," he said lamely.

"You see," Darlene crowed.

"Damn it, Darlene..." George growled.

"Now, now..." Earlene crooned.

Fred took the car out of automatic drive and put it into low gear, or sub-low gear, as he thought of it.

"The white stuff is getting deep," he muttered.

"What's that funny smell?" Earlene suddenly demanded.

"I smell it, too," Darlene said.

"Is the engine heating up, Fred?" George asked.

"A little bit... it's okay, though."

"I can't see a thing," Earlene whined.

"You brought boots, didn't you?" Darlene asked.

"Boots?"

"Jesus!" Fred swore.

"What is it, Fred?" Darlene and Earlene said in unison.

"The windshield wipers have stopped..."

6.

The car in which Keyes pulled up at Corinna's house was a 1980 Toyota Tercel. It had more rust on it than paint. The paint it did have was "burnt orange," or so a decorator or salesman might have described it; in fact, it was rust coloured. The body of the old vehicle was a Whistlerian study in rust-on-rust.

Corinna responded quickly to the pressure on her doorbell. She was wearing a leather coat, riding boots, a fur hat, and dark glasses. She looked to Keyes a bit like a Russian field marshal ready to defend Stalingrad. Her kit was stowed in a small rucksack, also leather.

"It's hideous," she said as she got into the Toyota. "Was this the best you could do?"

"No, Corinna. I started out with a Rolls, but this pathetic little fellow followed me home, so what could I do?" Then Keyes glared at her. "I *like* small cars, and the rental agency assured me—"

"But a Toyota?" Corinna interrupted. "I mean, really, an *orange* Toyota?"

"Listen," Keyes said, his exasperation growing, "if we're going to attempt this idiotic trip, you'll have to be nicer to me than that!"

Even Corinna could see the justice of this. She put her hand on his thigh.

"I'm sorry, Claude," she said sweetly. "I'll be *ever* so nice."

He glanced fiercely at the hand lying in his lap. "That's not what I meant."

"Fie, sir! Neither did I!"

"Until I find my way out of this doomed city," Keyes said gruffly, "please try to keep a civil tongue in your head."

"Not easy," Corinna said. "Not at all easy."

Keyes knew this for a true statement. He liked Corinna, admired her enormously, especially her unswerving dedication to books and those who created them. Keyes had often suspected the potential for even stronger feelings on his part— if not for the sharpness of her tongue, the ruthlessness of her invective, if not for her consuming need to win every argument, to always have the last word... if, if, if...

Anyway, Keyes was feeling more distant from Corinna than usual, because he was considering an uncomfortable solution to his driveway problem, should Marcia confirm the worst when he arrived in Stratford.

About a month earlier, he had received a proposal from a senior editor at one of Canada's largest publishers, a firm which Keyes, borrowing from Henry Miller, thought of as the Cosmodemonic Book Company. This editor had offered Keyes a work-for-hire project, the writing of the life story of Cosmodemonic's founder, a man whom Keyes couldn't be less interested in. What was unpalatable to Keyes was that the contract stipulated very firm guidelines as to how the book's subject was to be represented, the type of writing style to be used, what events in the man's life were to be ignored or glossed over, and so on. The publishers' proposed control over the text was so stringent, in fact, that Keyes figured if he agreed to their terms, he'd be little more than a stenographer taking dictation on a life from the subject himself.

Keyes was supremely bored by the very idea of biographing Mr. Cosmodemonic. He also hated being told what he could or could not write, and how to write it. Keyes had not officially turned down the proposal, but he planned to as soon as he was settled in Stratford.

Except that the contract offered a flat fee of thirteen thousand dollars in advance, payable upon signing the contract.

So, if push came to shove, Keyes could probably save his house— all it would cost him was his principles and self-respect. A further problem was that the closing was in two days— unless Marcia came up with further surprises— and he wouldn't get the money from Cosmodemonic for at least a week, even if he caved in.

He avoided thinking about the contempt such a semi-ghosted biography would draw down on him from Corinna Brand.

Keyes was so occupied with his dilemma that he did not really pay attention to how heavily the snow was falling as he felt his way through the traffic on Spadina toward the Gardiner Expressway, and grim points west.

7.

Despite the snow, the little Ministry of Transportation pickup truck continued on its way. The road was deserted now, or nearly so, but the working day was not yet done. Gordy Doig, the driver and man in command of the truck, decided to press on. His assistant, P.V. Choate, or Peavine, as he was universally known, was not so sanguine.

"We should go in now," Peavine growled.

"I hate turning back, Peavine. You know that."

"But it's getting worse, Gordy."

"I can still see the road," Gordy insisted, "and I still got radio contact..."

Gordy adjusted his headphones. He wore them over a military cap which had a "fifty-mission-crush" look about it. He rarely took the cap and headset off when he was driving, and sometimes left them on even when he got out of the truck. Then he would simply unplug the headset and go about with wires dangling; he loved his headphones.

"What do they say?"

"They say it's snowing," Gordy said after listening carefully for a few minutes.

"No shit?" said Peavine, unimpressed as usual by the wisdom that Gordy gleaned from his contacts with headquarters in Stratford.

"They say we should come in," Gordy added.

"Who you talking to?"

"Nobody... I'm just listening."

Peavine, who was not a patient man but made an attempt to be so in his dealings with Gordy, sighed and said: "Who you listening to, then?"

"Midge, I think. Maybe if Midge is there we should go in."

"Of course we should. It's snowing hard."

"They're calling for squalls..."

"They may be calling for squalls, but they're getting blizzard. Turn this bitch around."

"But it's only a mile or so to the West Dildo crossroad—"

"Too far."

"We can turn off there and double back..."

Peavine suddenly sat forward in his seat.

"Slow down, Gordy."

"Why? I don't see anything."

He did slow down, however, and, like Peavine, sat forward. Together they peered through the snow-fuddled windshield.

"There's something on the road," Peavine said.

"But I don't see anything..."

"Stop here." Peavine's tone of voice was as imperious as Caesar's might have been. "Stop, damnit!"

Gordy did. In the end, he always did what Peavine said, regardless of the fact that he, Gordy Doig, was in charge of the vehicle and their mission. Gordy had seniority. He had been working for the Ministry of Transportation since he was a boy just out of school. He had rarely missed a day that he hadn't intended to miss. Already he was talking about retirement, although he was still in his thirties. "I've seen too much death," he would say, shaking his head mournfully.

Peavine had been in government institutions for a long time, too, but mostly as a guest of the penal system. This Ministry job was the result of an experimental early-release work program brought in by the new administration. The project had recently been quietly dismantled after an indignant outcry from the public about giving jobs to convicts who hadn't even served their full sentences yet when so many honest and law-abiding people were out of work. Peavine was one of the last beneficiaries of the ill-timed program, and so far had stayed out of trouble. Beside not wishing to go back inside, this was the first regular employment he'd ever had which so perfectly suited his tastes and temperament.

"I *still* don't see a thing," Gordy said.

Peavine pulled up the hood of his parka and slipped his hands into his gloves. "Watch the door," he said.

He opened the door and got down. A frigid blast of wind caught the vehicle broadside. Before Peavine could slam the door shut, the cab took in a significant amount of snow.

"Shit!" Gordy said, brushing icy crystals out of his lap.

He watched between the frantic swipes of the windshield wipers as Peavine worked his way along the shoulder of the road. Peavine had a shovel in his hand and was hunched over almost double against the wind. Not for the first time, Gordy, who tended to think of everything in terms of animals, was fascinated by his partner's resemblance to some species of blond gorilla, especially bent over as he was so that his knuckles nearly scraped the snow. It was Gordy's most closely guarded secret, next to his moribund sex life, that he was mortally afraid of Peavine Choate.

"Not a damn thing," Gordy grumbled again.

But Peavine obviously had seen something. He stopped, squatted, made some brisk and strangely dramatic gestures. When he turned back toward the truck, he was dragging something behind him. Gordy felt the bed of the vehicle hop slightly behind him as Peavine threw whatever he was carrying into it.

The door opened and Peavine got in. More snow got in with him.

"What was it?" Gordy asked.

"Raccoon," Peavine explained. "A big boar 'coon."

"Dead?"

Peavine shook his head.

"Broken back, I think. Paralyzed." Then Peavine's beard split in the smile that always made Gordy think about making a will. "He's dead now."

Even though he had been on the roadkill patrol for a long time, Gordy never got used to that part of it. He could handle the dead ones, even the skunks, who were their best clients. But he hated finding the wounded ones, the maimed ones, the half-dead ones.

Peavine liked it.

"I didn't see him," Gordy mumbled a bit sheepishly.

"Neither did I," Peavine said, "but I knew he was there. Let's go in."

"Okay, Peavine. We'll go in."

8.

The orange Toyota attained the 401, principal automotive artery in that part of Canada and many other parts as well. Then they passed the airport. Because of the snow, the runways and hangars were relatively inactive, and no planes were taking off or landing. Visibility was not good. In fact, visibility was negligible, if not quite zero.

"All right, Brand," Keyes growled in his ineffective, if affectionate, Bogart voice, when they reached an unexpectedly snow-free stretch of highway. "What's so important?"

"It's the clown book."

"What?"

"Didn't I tell you I was working on a book about clowns?"

"Maybe you did..." Keyes muttered lamely.

"It's long overdue. There's a wealth of material, as they say, but it's never been assembled properly. There are books available, sure, but nothing really serious—"

"No *serious* books about clowns...?" Keyes mused aloud in mock disbelief.

Corinna ignored him. "— and there are individual chapters in books about the circus... Culhane gives good clown coverage, the best so far, I think, but he tries to encompass the whole spectacle. It's too much."

"And this book is focused on clowns?"

"Exactly."

"I still don't see why you have to race to Stratford with me." Or why it had to be *now*, in the middle of his crisis, Keyes finished silently. Of course, to be fair to Corinna, she had no idea that Keyes' crisis even existed; and he had no intention of telling her unless he absolutely had to.

"Because of Jonquil. Didn't I say that?"

Keyes shook his head. "What's a 'Jonquil?'"

"Jonquil is probably the greatest clown since Griebling and Lou Jacobs."

"I saw Jacobs when I was a kid."

"So did everybody. Well, Jonquil is in that class, and the really exciting thing is, Jonquil might be a Canadian!"

Keyes loved Canada, wouldn't live any place else, and made

no bones about saying so, but he had never been able to get excited about the game which Canadians played more enthusiastically than hockey or baseball, that is, the game Corinna was engaged in now, which he privately thought of as "Name that Canuck."

Corinna went on, "I know he spent several summers as a child in Ontario, a town called Cornerpost, which is just a few miles from Stratford. The book is already written, but there is the question of nationality—"

"We're driving a tin can through a blizzard so you can find out where a clown went to summer camp?"

"Not camp. There are no camps in Cornerpost. In fact, there's nothing much in Cornerpost; a few houses, a gas station, an abandoned railroad depot... He must have had family there."

"Must? Must?"

"All right, so I'm playing a hunch," Corinna said defensively.

"This is, of course, a dream," Keyes moaned.

"Shut up and drive, Claude."

Keyes did indeed shut up, wondering idly about clowns and editors, and the town of Cornerpost, Ontario.

9.

A motorcycle on the highway in weather such as this was unusual enough in itself. This particular cycle, and its rider, however, were even more anomalous. The rider's trim leather suit was of the type worn in professional motorcyle racing, all in white: boots, pants, jacket, and helmet. There were no insignia on the outfit, and only zippers, clasps, and snaps broke up its whiteness. The bike, a stripped down, powerful Yamaha, was also white, except for its chrome pipes and the matte black of its exposed mechanical parts. The motorcycle was almost invisible in the drifting snow.

The driver had called himself "Hawkwind" for so long he was no longer quite sure what name his parents had given him, nor the origin of the *nom de voyage* itself. He was just past twenty years old, but his skill with the machinery he straddled was evident by how little it skidded and swerved, considering the many ice patches on the highway and the increasingly heavy squalling of the snow through which he passed like a gasoline-driven ghost.

Anyone with experience at driving any vehicle at all in the Canadian winter would agree that Hawkwind's pale transit was both dangerous and insane.

The boy had to be one of the two.

10.

It was a mistake, Cassell thought, all a mistake.

His knuckles, gripping the steering wheel, were tense and as white as the night outside the car. He could see nothing through the storm but the bus's tail light, a dim red disk that faltered often to pink, to coral, or to nothingness.

I've got to make Jennet understand, he went on. I've got to try to make her understand.

A great gust of snow-laden wind engulfed the station wagon, cutting him off from everything, even the red will-of-the-wisp he was trying to follow.

"Christ!" Cassell said aloud. His hands trembled on the

wheel; the heavy car swerved, skidded, seeming about to spin away into the white chaos through which it was struggling.

The tail light reappeared, very close to him, too close. He stepped on the brakes, and again the vehicle swayed into a skid.

Again he managed to get out of it.

"Christ!" he whimpered. "Christ!"

Then there was something following him along the roadside— a group of people, dark and wildly gesticulating, he thought for an instant.

The windbreak of cedars held the snow in check, made it vault high over the road. It was like driving through a tunnel which penetrated the storm. Cassell could again see without straining, and now he could see more than the tail light; the whole rump of the bus was visible.

"Where the hell is it going?" Cassell demanded. He had entirely lost his bearings. It seemed hours since they had left Cornerpost... eons.

He glanced at the clock on the dashboard, then remembered that it had stopped, months before. He had meant to have it fixed, but...

It was too dark to see his watch and Cassell was afraid to take his hand off the wheel to put on the dome light.

It doesn't matter, he thought. Everyone will be late because of the snow.

He was thinking of his wife. She would be worried, but then, she was always worried. And in the end, it would be Jennet she would be concerned about, not him.

I've got to talk to Jennet, he thought. It will only take a minute or two. I'll apologize for frightening her, and I'll explain.

"It was a mistake," he said firmly. "She's got to understand that."

And she would understand, surely. He had never meant her any harm, hadn't meant to upset her. Besides, it was her fault.

One night he had come into his study well after midnight, to find Jennet sitting on his desk. Not on his chair at the desk, but on the desk. She was perched on a corner of it with her tight little bottom set squarely down among his budgets and voters' lists. To make matters worse, she was moving her right hand in the gesture which, for some unknown reason, always made Cassell tremble and perspire: to the right of Jennet's small, round, mouth was a tiny mole— a mark of beauty in some cultures, an "imperfection" in this one— which she absentmindedly stroked with a rotating motion of her index finger when she was distracted or nervous; on certain occasions she would also spend many minutes trying to cover it with make-up, one of her few affectations where her own appearance was concerned.

She was looking at the large map of pre-Confederation Canada displayed beside his blackboard; despite his early retirement to enter local politics, Cassell still thought of himself primarily as a history teacher.

"Nice map, Burgess," Jennet had said, turning and staring at him as squarely as she sat on his papers.

"Why didn't I throw her out?" he asked himself now, or asked the storm howling about and above him. "Why didn't I stop it as soon as it started?"

But he knew the answer: he didn't stop her because he had liked her calling him Burgess. It diminished the chasm of years between them. He didn't stop her because he liked the lines and curves of her body draped artlessly across his desk.

"But was she putting me on?" That would be like her. That was the reputation she had. In her own peculiar way, she was known as a troublemaker, not openly, but in some covert, nonconformist way. Her teachers complained that she had no respect for them, did not take them seriously. They didn't like her much.

She was, however, bright, even "gifted," in the jargon of the pedagogical world. Jennet got excellent marks in the classes she attended— she was a notorious hookey player, so everyone knew when she was bored by a particular class or teacher.

And she had no close friends. Unlike the other girls in her class, and the boys too, Jennet was comfortable being by herself. She didn't show up at sporting events; she didn't go to dances; she didn't hang out at the usual hang-out spots, smoking and trying to look tough.

Why her? During all his years standing in classes before hundreds of young girls as pretty as Jennet, with their short skirts and tight tank tops and their easy attitude towards their own new sexuality, not once had there been a hint of impropriety in his treatment of them. He had not even really noticed the little tramps... So, why Jennet? She was his stepdaughter, after all, and, with her malcontent ways and bright mind, she was trouble.

She had called him Burgess.

11.

The Ministry vehicle was in four-wheel drive and moving very slowly. Blowing snow made the road difficult, often impossible, to see. Gordy Doig was grumbling and cursing under his breath.

"I guess you were right, Peavine," Gordy said. "I guess we should have gone in an hour ago."

"I know we should have."

"I'd better call in."

"What for?"

"Let them know where we are."

"Oh, good idea, Gordy— where are we?"

Gordy gaped. "I thought you'd know..."

"I do... more or less. We haven't got to West Dildo yet... or if we have, I didn't see it go by. But then, I can't see shit."

"I'll call in." Gordy lifted his microphone, then fiddled with the dials on the dashboard. "Hello, Midge. Come in, Midge. Can you read me, Midge?"

"....."

"Ten-four, Midge. We're still out here, close to West Dildo, Peavine says."

"....."

"I know, Midge, but it didn't look so bad then—"

"....."

"No, we haven't seen anybody else. Picked up a raccoon a ways back, but—"

"....."

"An accident, you say?" He turned to Peavine. "Midge says there's been a big accident on the 401. Closed in both directions."

"Keep your eyes on the road, Gordy."

"Right, Peavine. What's that, Midge? Re-routing all the traffic—"

"....."

"Out this way? We haven't seen a soul."

"Out this way?" Peavine echoed. "What good's that going to do?"

"Highway's closed, detour through—" He broke off. "Through where?" He spoke again into the microphone. "Where did you say, Midge? What's that? Midge!"

"What's the matter?"

"I lost her. The radio cut out. I *told* Etherington a hundred times we needed a new radio." Gordy twiddled his dials, cursed again. "Nothing! I put an official requisition in and everything, and you know what Etherington said?" Peavine looked as if he really didn't give a hoot in hell what Etherington said, but Gordy went on anyway, his small round face reddening. "Etherington said that sure we could have a new radio, but with all the government cuts to the budget, he'd have to make the money up by cutting *my* hours! And now look what's happened. Biggest blizzard of the year, and I can't even talk to Midge!"

"It doesn't make much difference, does it? Midge isn't exactly going to come get us, is she?"

"No, but..."

"Look at that, Gordy— car up ahead, I think..."

Gordy peered through his icy windshield.

"I don't see..."

"There— there, in the ditch!"

"I better stop, Peavine."

"What if you can't get her going again?"

"Somebody might be hurt!"

Peavine grumbled. Gordy stopped the truck. Peavine reluctantly pulled up his parka, put on his gloves and opened the door.

"Jee-zus, Peavine! Close it!"

Peavine hunched his shoulders and battled into the storm. Then he disappeared in it.

It was several minutes before the door opened again. Peavine, totally encased in snow, crawled into the cab.

"Almost lost you, Gordy. Can't see a thing out there."

"What about the car?"

"In the ditch, all right... big bitch."

"Yes, but— ?"

"Nobody in it. Looks like they decided to go for a walk."

"They? Why *they*?"

"Lots of luggage. I think they started taking their stuff with them. They couldn't get far."

"Maybe we'll find them up ahead."

"Yeah... doing popsicle imitations!" This thought did not seem all that disturbing to Peavine.

12.

Louise De Wetering was a big woman who enjoyed being in motion, and so her profession of commercial bus driver fit her as comfortably as her favourite pair of blue jeans. She relished and took pride in all aspects of her work: controlling the huge vehicle, the responsibility of transporting people to their destinations, the hours— everything, in fact, except the sometimes grim dangers of storms like the one she was now slowly and carefully guiding the bus through. It was mildly comforting to have only two quiet, well-behaved passengers to consider, although she took their safety as seriously as that of a full load; it was simply much easier for Louise to concentrate on the road when there were no drunks or wailing babies or worse to contend with.

She glanced into the mirror above her: the man sat strumming his guitar so softly that she couldn't even hear it above the engine and the wind; the young girl— sixteen at most, Louise guessed— was asleep in her seat, as she had been since shortly after boarding at Cornerpost. Louise allowed herself a moment of wistful envy at the thought of being that young and carefree; the kid was probably on her way to some doting grandparents, or somewhere equally idyllic and undemanding...

At the back of the bus, Jennet moaned softly in her sleep, dreaming of where she was going, and of where she had been: she was floating in an iron-grey sky, while, in the bilocation of dream, she was also watching herself running across a field of ice, except that the fleeing figure was doing more slipping and falling than actual running. Jennet-above shifted her point of view to try and see what or who Jennet-below was running from; she saw a giant, disembodied face, wavering as if seen through water, speeding low over the ice towards Jennet-who-ran, who had tumbled to the ground. Jennet-who-watched smiled as she recognized the source of the image: it was from her favourite movie, *The Wizard of Oz*, the projection of The Great and Powerful Oz himself, used by the little man from Kansas to frighten Dorothy. Then the scene blinked and there was only one Jennet, struggling to get back up on her feet. She could not quite do so, and craned her head to see that her pursuer was almost directly overhead. It was not the basically gentle face of Professor Marvel, but that of her stepfather, Burgess Cassell. Jennet began to cry, not out of fear but out of frustration at being unable to stand, at being helpless before this absurd manifestation. Then there was a voice, neither Cassell's nor Marvel's. It was a woman's voice, and Jennet saw a second face appear, opposite the first one. The new face was in repose, eyes closed, mouth relaxed as in sleep. The voice belonged to this strange, but strangely familiar, woman, although the lips did not move: "Pay no attention to that man behind the curtain. Pay no attention to that man..."

"... pay no attention... no attention," Jennet mumbled as she shifted into a more comfortable position in the cramped confines of the bus seat. The man across the aisle from her watched the girl's face become less tense, and she began to snore, a low, regular purring sound. He executed the last few notes of a countrified interpretation of "Somewhere Over the Rainbow," then set his instrument aside and stood, his long legs creaking as they unfolded. He walked easily to the front of the bus, as if long accustomed to navigating around moving vehicles.

"How're we doin'?" he asked Louise, who removed her right hand from the steering wheel and waggled it in a universal gesture which meant "six of one, half-a-dozen of the other," not taking her eyes from the road.

"We be in Stratford soon? I got a gig tonight."

"We're as close to Stratford as we're going to get for a while," Louise answered. "Right on the edge of town, but the plows haven't been through here yet, so I'm not going any further. I'm going to pull in at a motel up ahead. I know the people who run it." She pointed to a blue light winking intermittently through the snow off the vehicle's starboard side. "End of the line."

"Well, I guess I could walk to the Wabash..."

"Where?"

"Place I'm supposed to play– The Wabash-Canon Bar & Grill. Al Wabash is an old acquaintance of mine; never met his partner, Canon, far as I know."

Louise removed her cap, shaking out her long red hair. "Never heard of it. Must be new. Anyway, I don't think you'd get twenty yards in this. Say, is that kid still asleep?"

"I think so. Want me to get her up?"

"Well, we don't want her to freeze to death, and it's going to get cold in here as soon as I turn the engine off."

Together they went back for Jennet, who was curled up like a sleeping cat around her black bag. Her hair spilled down over her face, covering her features like a vestal's veil.

"Come on, kid," the man said. "Wake up."

Jennet straightened abruptly, then shrank down even further into her seat as she saw the two faces looming above her. Her eyes were very wide.

"It's all right, honey," Louise said. "The storm's getting worse. We're going to have to stay here for a while."

Jennet looked out the window.

"Where are we?"

"Stratford, almost."

Immediately Jennet stood up, pushed her hair out of her eyes and gathered her bag into her arms.

"I'm ready."

The three travellers left the bus and trudged through the mounting drifts and falling snow toward the blurred blue light.

13.

The bus pulled off the road, and Cassell followed it. When it stopped, he did too, although he was confused. The bus seemed to have come to rest in the middle of a white nowhere. Then, about fifty yards or so ahead of him, he saw the vague outline of a building looming out of the milky maelstrom into which he had been sucked.

Cassell turned off the car's ignition and sat quietly for a while. Steadily and rapidly the storm began to build a white cocoon up about the vehicle, about him.

He was warm enough still, but he supposed the warmth

wouldn't last long now that the heater was silent. But for now he was comfortable. He was also very tired.

Cassell closed his eyes and snuggled deeper into his duffle coat.

The snow drifted up about the driver's side of the car, the north side, Cassell supposed. Oddly enough that was all he supposed about the drifting snow. And yet, somehow, he knew it would be the death of him if he didn't do something to escape. That something, whatever it was, should be done soon, if it was to be done at all.

"Too tired," he told himself. Then, snuggling more deeply into his coat: "Too comfy."

It was a word his wife used: "... comfy..."

Bibsy would be angry; not just worried, but furious.

He wondered why. She certainly didn't want him at home. She needed him, of course, but only to pay the bills, and to keep her from appearing unsupported.

She didn't care for him, never had cared much, but she cared about being married. The married state was the only one to which she had ever aspired, and she clung to it like lint to velvet, like death to life.

Although she never admitted it, he knew that she wished she was clinging to that state with someone other than him.

Bibsy! Why on earth should a forty-three-year-old woman be called Bibsy? Why should anyone be called Bibsy?

Why do I call her Bibsy? Cassell demanded angrily of himself. What's wrong with Barbara?

There was nothing wrong with Barbara, he knew, but his wife was not a Barbara. Regardless of her christening, she was a Bibsy.

The greatest of his problems, his confusions, was that there wasn't really anything wrong with Bibsy, nothing that he could demonstrate, even to himself. She was pretty enough. She had kept her figure trim by playing golf. She looked after the house. She shopped and cooked and, when she had to, entertained his political colleagues.

She even made some money, doing part-time work at the local newspaper. She was a good typist and a good enough grammarian to edit copy. Cassell had no idea how much money she was paid for her work at the *Cornerpost Courier*. That was her money. His salary, on the other hand, was their money. Not that he cared. They had enough to support the life they had fashioned for themselves.

"And we make love twice a month," Cassell grumbled. The euphemism "make love" grated on his nerves. "She lets me fuck her twice a month," he bitterly corrected.

He no longer tried to convince himself that she enjoyed these encounters. In the early years of their marriage, she had pretended to some pleasure, but, as he eventually learned, it was only because she so desperately wanted a child to complete her vision of the married state, of the perfect family to replace the flawed one from which she had escaped by marrying Burgess. Those years of feigned happiness were no more. *Lost in the mists of time*, as he sometimes said in his speeches on the decline of families and values.

It was Bibsy's fault, too. It was her need for some sort of motherhood which had led to the adoption of Jennet; the two women had conspired against him in some estrogen-based way which he was ill-equipped to understand.

"Mists of time..." he droned sleepily. "Snows of yesteryear..."

The snows of now relentlessly continued their work on the white sarcophagus building about Burgess Cassell's car.

14.

"Quaeris, quot mihi basiationes... tuae, Lesbia, sint satis super-que?"[1]

"Oh, can it for once, will you, Oswald? You know I'm not Lesbia. My name's Belle. And you aren't Catullus, for Christ's sake. Cut it out."

The small woman who called herself Belle stepped behind the counter and thumped the old-fashioned cash register with peevish determination. Bells rang and a drawer slid open. Belle dipped into it and took out a meager clutch of bills.

"We'd be just as well off if we closed right down at this time of year," she said.

There was no one in the room with her, a largish room with tables and chairs and benches and booths. Nevertheless, she spoke. And was answered from the kitchen, which communicated with the restaurant by a square window fitted with a small counter instead of a proper sill, by a clatter of pots and pans. It was more than a random clatter of the sort that is made by cooking or washing up. It was deliberate and almost, but not quite, musical. Someone in the kitchen was beating out responses on metal vessels with a pair of spoons, one metal and one wooden.

"I'm serious, Oswald," Belle went on. "We don't make enough money in the winter to pay the hydro bills. There hasn't been a soul in all day."

Rat-a-tat-tat... bong! replied the kitchen percussionist.

---

1. "Lesbia, you want to know how many kisses are more than enough?"

"Close up and go to Florida, that's what I'd like to do."

Bong! and again: *Bong!*

Then a man's voice, the one that had spoken in Latin earlier, said: "O uenusta Sirmio..."[2]

Belle laughed. "All right. Sirmio, if you want, wherever that is. Do you suppose we could hitch a ride with a trucker all the way to Sirmio? We could to Florida. Homer Matz said he'd take us next trip he makes. He'd do it, too. Homer's a good guy and he's not even trying to get into my pants."

Rat-a-tat-tat... tat... tat... tat. The sound dwindled to pianissimo at the end.

"At least I don't think he is," Belle added.

"Dicebas quondam solum te nosse Catullum... Lesbia, nec prae me uelle tenere Iouem..."[3]

"Belle! *Not* Lesbia, and I don't know what the hell you're talking about. I took the damned course, took it all the way through fucking Caesar, but I didn't get to Catullus. You know I didn't even get to Cicero, so I can't understand—"

"Huc est mens deducta tua, mea Lesbia, culpa... atque ita se officio perdidit ipsa suo... ut iam nec bene uelle queat tibi, si optima fias... nec desistere amare, omnia si facias..."[4]

"Oswald, please— stop," Belle said. There were tears in her

---

2. "Sweet Sirmio..."

3. "You told me I was the only one, Lesbia, you wanted me more than Jupiter himself."

4. "Lesbia, I'm so down and it's all your fault. I'm so lost on account of you. If you were the best of women I couldn't wish you well. I can't stop loving you no matter what I do."

voice. "I try... I try to understand what you're saying or trying to say, but I get very tired."

She waited, but there was no sound from the kitchen.

"Oh, why can't you speak to me in plain Canadian?"

"Odi et amo... odi et amo..."[5]

Belle put her face in her hands.

"Please, Oswald," she murmured, "no more tonight... no more..."

"Odi et amo... odi et amo..."

Suddenly furious, Belle bent forward and shrieked through the window into the kitchen. "No more, I said!"

All was quiet in the kitchen.

"Not another fucking word, unless... unless it's in some language I can understand!"

Still the kitchen was quiet, so Belle turned back to her work of counting up the week's receipts.

"That can't be all," she murmured. She searched deeper in the drawer, and came across a small, nickel-plated revolver, which she took out and put on the counter.

"Why do I keep this dumb thing? It scares me every time I catch sight of it," she said.

Then she dug still deeper into the darkest recesses of the cash register.

In the kitchen, pots rattled very gently, making a slow drum roll, faint as distant thunder, not ominous like the thunder of a storm approaching, but melancholic, like that of a storm fading away.

---

5. "I hate and I love."

15.

Hazy blue lights began to flicker uncertainly in the sky ahead and above the Toyota, barely visible through gusting sheets of heavy snow. Oh, good, Keyes thought, UFOs. First the highway had become all but impassable as the gentle snow transformed to storm then to blizzard, and they had detoured at the first likely turnoff, in accordance with the radio's highway-report instructions. All well and good, but then Corinna had convinced Keyes, against his better judgement, to detour even further, on the basis of a road sign, which, Keyes had to admit, he might have been tempted by under better driving conditions. The opportunity to visit WEST DILDO 10 KM would have been too good to pass up.

But sightseeing in this frost-giant's paradise would be foolish, if not suicidal. The forecast for the evening now included temperatures in the minus thirties Celsius, with the wind chill factor; frostbite warnings were in effect. Corinna, however, was enjoying herself immensely, mostly at Keyes' expense.

"See?" she said. "If you'd taken up cross-country skiing last winter like I suggested, this would be a piece of cake!"

"A frozen piece of cake," Keyes said. With true gentlemanly restraint, he refrained from reminding Corinna that her own experience with said sport had in fact consisted of only two chastening outings, although he was sure that in her own mind she was a seasoned veteran. "Can you make out what those lights are?"

Corinna leaned forward to squint out through the windshield.

"I think it's a neon sign," she said after a moment. "Yeah, it is; it says Blue... you. Blue You? What the hell is that supposed to mean?"

"Maybe it's some kind of sanatorium for manic-depressives," Keyes suggested, but as they crawled slowly closer, the rest of the sign, obscured by snow and several burned out bulbs, became visible: BLUE BAYOU MOTEL & DINER. Beneath the electrical display, in less gaudy raised letters of metal, was the notice: ROOMS AVAILABLE IN SEASON.

Sure hope we're in season, Keyes thought as he pulled up in front of the roadhouse, beside several other vehicles in various stages of ivory burial, including a Cha-Co Trails bus and, incongruously under the circumstances, a muscular-looking motorcycle.

"Nice bike," Keyes muttered. "Yamaha 750 Special."

Corinna raised an eyebrow.

"How do you know that?"

"Research," Keyes answered. "Wait a minute! I remember this place– we're right outside Stratford. I'll be damned. Shall we?"

The door was only a few yards from where they had parked, but both were covered in snow by the time they reached it. Bells tinkled overhead as they stepped into moist warmth and noisy confusion, to which they added briefly by stamping and shaking the snow from their persons.

Keyes had never actually been inside the Blue Bayou before, having only passed by it on numerous occasions years earlier, when he had worked at the Shakespearean Festival. It seemed to him that it had been called something else then. Based on the current name, he had been vaguely expecting some kind of pseudo-Cajun decor, stuffed gators or crayfish nets and the sort of diluted Louisiana funk he had seen on occasion in certain

Toronto establishments, but a quick glance indicated that there was, in fact, no attempt at any kind of decor at all, unless it was Early American Truckstop. A formica-topped counter ran half the length of the long room, fronted by red leatherette stools which were bolted to the linoleum floor. Past the counter at chest height was a large window which opened into the kitchen. Several booths flanked each side of the door, more red leather and formica. A large booth, in the shape of a horseshoe, dominated the wall to Keyes' right, a juke box beside it. Keyes noticed that each booth was equipped with a chrome and glass juke box slave mechanism, so that songs could be played without leaving the safety of one's table. Menus and placards with homely aphorisms lined the walls, along with other signs, among them the essential and comforting WASHROOMS, with an arrow pointing to a corridor beside the swinging doors to the kitchen. About a dozen people sat or milled about, no doubt fellow refugees from the sudden storm.

"Well, don't just stand there with your teeth in your mouth, you two!" bellowed a woman's voice from behind the counter. "Coffee's free, everything else is half price for the duration of the hostilities!"

The words "free coffee" were enough to set Keyes moving in the direction of the offer, Corinna at his heels. As they approached the proffered pot, Keyes swept the room with a quick glance, storing first impressions of its occupants, "collecting characters," he called it; unlike many other writers who worked in non-fiction, Keyes did not have several chapters of The Great Canadian Novel tucked away in a secret drawer. He was, however, a great fan of short fiction, and thought that one day he might take a shot at writing it himself. Against that time, he had built up a small but select mental file of persons, places, and situations which he thought might prove useful to such an undertaking.

There was certainly some variety here, he thought, as he completed his brief inventory: at the large booth was a quartet of older people, two men and two women, stunningly ordinary except for the garish unsuitability of their summer clothing; they kept glancing nervously at the young man dressed in white leather who sat cross-legged on the floor beside the juke box; although the juke box was not playing, the youth nodded his head of wild dreadlocks back and forth in time to music that Keyes could not hear; at one end of the counter, three people in uniform were huddled together in earnest discussion in which the word "storm" figured prominently— one of them, a big, redheaded woman in a grey uniform, was definitely the driver of the bus. The others were in road-workers' gear of some kind.

The circus of human diversity was definitely in town, Keyes decided as he and Corinna gratefully accepted two cups of steaming coffee and sat down at the counter. Beside Keyes was a teenaged girl in black, hunched over her own coffee so that her long fair hair obscured her face; earplug wires travelled from beneath the hair to a Walkman on the counter beside her saucer, precluding an attempt at introduction. Keyes turned his attention to their hostess, who was already attempting to refill the cup from which he had barely sipped. She was a woman of medium height and indeterminate age. Her hair, tightly bound into a ponytail, was of the same colour as the girl's, but a strand or two of grey gave away the colour's Clairol origin. The tiny lines around her eyes and mouth, poorly concealed by a mask of make-up, announced that this lady was older in either years or experience than she wished the world at large to know. A tag on her dark blue waitress's uniform read "Belle," a name Keyes had never encountered in life, but by which he was immediately charmed.

"Drink up, sweetie!" Belle ordered. "There's a fresh pot

brewing, and something tells me it's gonna be a long night!" She turned away to the service window behind her; Keyes nodded in appreciation of a slim body, small of breast and thigh, but with long, powerful legs which suggested many years of endless journeys between counter and table. "Oswald!" she called into what Keyes could now see was indeed the kitchen, "Did you bring more coffee out of storage yet?"

There was a clatter of metal in answer, and what may or may not have been a grunt of human origin. Belle shook her head in exasperation.

"Well, shake a leg!" She aimed a scarlet smile at Corinna. "Men! Can't live with 'em, can't sell 'em on the open market!"

"Oh, I don't know about that," Corinna said with an answering grin. "I got a pretty good offer on Claude here recently, and believe me, he's got a lot of wear and tear on him..."

Belle leaned over to squint at Keyes, as people whose vision is poor but refuse to wear glasses sometimes do. "Honey, he's all right— he just doesn't eat enough. Got some fresh coconut-cream pie that might fix that."

"Maybe later," Keyes said with a grimace as he stood up; his aversion to coconut was little known, but profound. "Right now I need to use your phone and your washroom. Feel free to continue talking amongst yourselves while I'm gone."

"Phone's out, sweetie," Belle called after him. "Must be the storm. Bathroom still works, though."

Keyes frowned in frustration. He was eager to reach Marcia and find out how the land, or rather the driveway, lay.

He nodded to the uniformed trio as he passed them, still much involved in weather prognostication at the end of the counter, then nearly stumbled over an obstruction which he had not noticed before: a black guitar case and a pair of black-booted feet. A tall and gaunt man was leaning against the wall in the shadows of the corridor which led to the bathrooms. His face was mostly obscured by dark glasses and a large dark hat. He turned the head slightly toward Keyes and spoke in a deep, gravel-strewn voice.

"Don't much mind about the feet, friend, but I'd appreciate it if you'd be careful of Ivy..."

"Ivy?" Keyes asked, looking around for another person.

The man's head shifted again, in the direction of the instrument case.

"Oh," Keyes said. "Sorry."

During the brief exchange, the dark man's hands had moved quickly and efficiently between his pocket and a small leather pouch; the end result was a perfectly rolled cigarette, which he lit with a wooden match scraped against the panelling. He extended the pouch toward Keyes.

"Smoke?"

Keyes had recently succeeded in giving up cigarettes yet again, and knew what such a rough construct would do to his throat, but was hesitant to refuse this oblique acknowledgment of his apology for interfering with Ivy.

"Thanks, not right now... I, uh, have to see a man about a horse," he answered, pleased at remembering this antiquated phrase from his college years.

Ivy's owner nodded, then leaned back into his lurking position against the wall, accepting the conclusion of this small masculine ritual. Keyes continued to a door marked DUDES; its neighbour read DAMES. "What circle of purgatory have I stumbled into?" Keyes muttered as he entered. The bathroom was scrupulously clean: sinks and urinals were pristine white, the metal fixtures sparkled silver, and the walls were painted a subdued and mottled blue, an effect Keyes recognized as having been achieved by daubing a large sponge over fresh paint; there was a faint scent of roses in the air, almost successfully masking the sharp odour of antiseptic. He remembered then that the restaurant itself, while primitive, was equally scrubbed and polished.

Keyes attended to his immediate needs, then, as he stood at the sink splashing cold water onto his face, it struck him that his first impressions of the Blue Bayou's current clientele might be grossly unfair. Keyes had spent the greater part of his life either alone with his books and music, or surrounded by entertainers, actors, and dancers, and the last five years in the insular world of small-press publishing, a hermetic and incestuous environment if there ever was one. Even his recent social outing at The Rhinestone Cowperson had not exactly been an evening among the rank-and-file of the working class. The people in the restaurant beyond the door were probably, after all, simply "real people," with respectable, necessary jobs, uncomplicated by the often neurotic, often pretentious concerns of that section of the Canadian populace which Keyes knew best, those who had committed themselves to the insecure vocations of art, literature, and entertainment.

"Have you become an elitist, Keyes?" he asked his reflection.

The image in the mirror shrugged, but gave no opinion one way or another.

16.

During Keyes' absence, the situation in the dining room had livened up. He stood again beside the tall man (avoiding Ivy's toes), watching a confrontation between the four older people and the motorcyclist. The young man stood beside the booth with his head cocked to one side, while the two women spoke simultaneously and loudly; the men at the table sat with heads bowed, their faces red with either embarrassment or anger.

"He didn't mean anything. *I* think your hair is very... interesting," insisted one woman.

"It's just that we aren't in the company of many young people," said the other. "George didn't mean to insult you..."

The white-garbed rider cocked his head to the other side, as if considering this explanation, then walked in a tight circle, finally facing George again, who did not look in the least bit contrite or apologetic. When the young man spoke, it was with an accent that sounded to Keyes' ear like a West Indian rhythm, but learned second hand, as if from television.

"That," said the youth, pointing a finger at George, "got to be the ugliest shirt I ever seen!"

George began to stand, followed slowly by Fred.

"Now just a damn minute—"

The tall man beside Keyes straightened.

"Goddamn fools," he muttered, stepping forward. "Let's go, friend."

Keyes assumed that it was he and not the guitar who was being addressed, and began to follow with somewhat the same reluctance as Fred was showing in backing up George.

Why couldn't we have been snowed in with the Von Trapp family, or The Brady Bunch? Keyes thought as they approached the knot of angry people. Then he sighed under his breath, supposing that such a situation would have been equally annoying, in its own way. You get what you get, he decided, as he and the big man stopped between the Cooks and the Bakers, and the biker.

"Name's McKendricks," said Keyes' new friend as he reached across to grip George Cook's hand in what at first appeared to be a simple handshake, but Keyes noticed a look of distress cross George's face as his hand was squeezed; George sat back down quickly. "Is there a problem here?"

Satisfied that this side of things was being looked after, Keyes turned to face the young man, who did not look upset or frightened, just puzzled.

"That your bike outside?" Keyes asked. Hawkwind nodded, or rather, bobbed his head up and down enthusiastically. "Weather's a bit nasty for riding, isn't it?"

Hawkwind grinned in a lopsided but engaging fashion, and the bobbing head shifted from up and down to side to side.

"Better this way," he said in his off-kilter accent. "More dangerous... more fun."

"I guess it would be. I'm Claude Keyes." This introduction brought no response, so Keyes stuck out his hand. "And you are—?"

The youth adopted what to Keyes looked like a well-practised pose, legs apart, hands on hips.

"The storm riders of the frozen night call me Hawkwind!"

O-kay, Keyes thought, lowering his hand. There was a look in Hawkwind's eyes that was as indecipherable as his accent, and Keyes was not at all sure that he wanted to investigate it further. Anyway, a potentially ugly situation seemed to have been defused.

He turned to see how McKendricks was making out.

"We may be here a while," he was saying in a reasonable voice, "and we don't have to like each other, but being civil doesn't cost anything, right?"

George did not look as if he necessarily agreed (nor did Fred, for that matter), but said nothing, glowering instead at the juke mechanism, and flipping its selection plates with his left hand.

"Good. Glad we're all in accord," McKendricks concluded, then turned to Hawkwind. "Goes for you, too, son." Then, to Keyes, "Buy you a cup of coffee?"

"Certainly, Mr. McKendricks," Keyes agreed, falling in step behind him to the counter.

"You can call me Joe— Moanin' Joe, if you like, but that's really just my stage name."

"Joe it is. Jean-Claude Keyes, but Claude is what I go by."

"Pleasure, J.C."

"Same to you." *J.C.?!* Terrific, Keyes thought.

Corinna was staring at them, as everyone else had been during the brief scene, but the others had returned to their conversations and cups of coffee as soon as it was obvious that no blood would be spilled. Joe tipped his hat to her in as old-fashioned a manner as Keyes had seen in some time.

"This is my friend, Corinna Brand," Keyes said. "Corinna, Moanin' Joe McKendricks."

To Keyes' surprise, Corinna acknowledged McKendricks with only the curtest of nods, then resumed whatever conversation she had struck up with Belle. In an attempt to cover a certain amount of embarrassment and confusion, Keyes began to babble.

"Corinna and I work together... she's an editor, I write, and we, uh, she's doing some research in this area, and I'm in the middle of moving here from Toronto... then the storm hit...

It's..." Keyes ran out of words very quickly, since he really had nothing to say.

"I wrote a book once," said McKendricks, nodding slowly.

"Really!" Keyes breathed a silent sigh of relief, relief which quickly turned to curiosity. "What kind of book?"

"Book about Tom Connors, about his songs really. Paid to have it printed myself. Didn't sell many." McKendricks shrugged. "Didn't much care. Tom and some of his family liked it. Got one review— guy said I should pay more attention to dotting the *i*'s and stroking the *t*'s, or some such thing. Probably right. You know anything about music, J.C.?"

"Not that kind... but I seem to be learning about it," Keyes laughed, remembering the movie-western ambience of The Rhinestone Cowperson, and trying to imagine Moanin' Joe among that gentle but fey herd of gay urban cowfolk, with their general attitude of "Show Tunes at the OK Corral."

"Well, can't hurt you." McKendricks said.

"I suppose not."

Belle approached them with her everpresent pot of coffee, and filled their cups.

"Thanks for stepping in, fellas," she said, setting creamers and sugar packets beside their mugs. "I didn't want to have to call Oswald— he hates leaving the kitchen; makes him mean. Somebody might have got the business end of a meat tenderizer upside the head! Not that some people don't need a good smack every now and then to remind them we're all human beings!"

Keyes watched as McKendricks blithely ripped open and emptied six sugar envelopes into his coffee, ignoring the cream. McKendricks noticed Keyes' consternation. He did not exactly smile, but he looked a hair less grim as he lifted the mug to clink against Keyes' own.

"Black as hell, sweet as love," he said, and drank deeply, with the restrained enthusiasm of a man who thoroughly enjoyed his coffee, and perhaps his entire life.

17.

Burgess Cassell roused himself at last from the drowsy comfort which had enveloped him, and snapped open the glove compartment, hoping that he had not drained his reserves during the last town council meeting. No, there it was, the reassuring feel of the squarish pint of medicinal gin, which he saw was still only half-empty when he held the green glass up to his eyes.

The lemony vapours and a substantial gulp dispelled the chill from his body and the warm fuzziness from his mind. The building a hundred yards beyond was visible every few minutes, appearing and disappearing as if behind a white curtain which opened or closed depending on the whimsy of the wind, and Cassell frowned as a knot of tension began to form deep in his gut: did he know this place...?

A demanding whirlwind of gin-scented memory surged to the forefront of his consciousness, replacing the exterior storm, and Burgess Cassell saw in frightening detail the Emerald Isle Motor Inn, as this establishment had been known seventeen years before. It had been a holiday weekend, and the occasion a yearly convention of the fraternal order to which Cassell belonged, one whose members sponsored various worthy charities and community events when they were not wearing outlandish headgear and participating in jealously guarded rituals whose pagan origins had long been buried behind a veneer of Christian sentiment and middle-class respectability.

Stratford had been chosen as the site of the convention because of its excellent tourist-support infrastructure, and because some of the brethren enjoyed taking in a play or two (when not drinking heavily or playing practical jokes on one another), especially at the substantial discount rate given to organizations such as theirs. Cassell himself didn't mind sitting through one of Shakespeare's History plays, mostly because he enjoyed pointing out what he perceived as the production's inaccuracies and anachronisms.

They had convened on a beautiful weekend in early summer, he recalled. The Emerald Isle was surrounded by greenery and bathed in golden sunlight, and from the moment he arrived, Cassell contrived to forget that he was married. He drank too much, he talked too much and too loudly, and his eyes never left the various young women who worked as waitresses and chambermaids. Several of his co-conventioneers remarked at how different Cassell seemed from the staid and stuffy Cornerpost schoolteacher who had boarded the bus with them on Friday. Although, they observed, he was no less pompous for all his born-again-bachelor posturing.

Of course— as he was fond of reminding himself in years to come— he'd had no intention of being unfaithful to Barbara. "It just happened," was his favourite self-justification for the event. On Sunday morning, the last official day of the convention, he had overslept because of a spectacular hangover, and had forgotten to hang the DO NOT DISTURB sign on the door. Coming out of the bathroom, he was greeted by the sight of a tight-skirted and unmistakably female bottom; the chambermaid was bent over his bed, restoring it to order. Dark blonde hair hung down over her shoulder in a long ponytail, and she straightened up in surprise at the sound of the bathroom door closing. When she turned, Cassell saw that there were tears streaming down her young and attractive face.

"Sorry..." she began, then convulsed in a fresh attack of crying.

"Are you all right, miss?" he asked, moving toward her, having momentarily forgotten that he was clad in only a bright yellow terrycloth towel, a towel which did little to hide certain aspects of Cassell's sudden interest in the weeping chambermaid. Then, as he got closer to her, Cassell realized that not only was she crying, she was also slightly unsteady on her feet, and there was a heavy smell of gin in the air.

"Fucker had no right to dump me!" she wailed. Then she fell or tripped forwards into Cassell's arms. Her next words were muffled by Cassell's damp shoulder. "I'll show him..."

Cassell smiled to himself, thinking how rarely in a man's life such an opportunity came along. The girl needed comforting, after all, and no one would be hurt by his offering her a little affection. As he mumbled soothing phrases into her ear, he realized that the girl was very drunk, indeed: she was using him for support more than anything else. He steered her toward the bed, kissing her smooth neck and running one hand lightly along her breast.

"You're far too good for him," (whoever "him" might be) Cassell whispered as he unbuttoned her uniform, interpreting her lack of struggle as consent, although she did little to aid in his efforts. She did manage a slurred giggle when he pricked himself on the pin of her nameplate, which he could not read without his eyeglasses. After that she made only the occasional sound which was either a sob or a snore.

She was deeply asleep the moment Cassell rolled away from her, and he left her that way. As he dressed, Cassell immediately began the process of separating himself from the encounter, pretending it had never happened. He gathered his things together and checked out of the motel without saying goodbye to his fellows or looking back. Over the years, whenever the memory of the Emerald Isle blindsided him, it was always accompanied by fear. Fear that the girl (by now a woman) would track him down, would show up on his doorstep demanding reparation or acknowledgment of some sort, or, worse yet, that some teenaged boy would accost him and insist on his paternity. There would go his political career, and possibly his marriage. Such as it was.

Cassell forced himself back to the present, and he shuddered, taking a burning slug of gin to settle his anxiety. So much like Jennet, that long-ago girl had been, now that he came to think of her again.

So much like Jennet...

18.

Belle had been explaining that their units were all vacant, it being the off-season, and that everyone was welcome to the rooms at a much-reduced storm rate whenever they were ready to bunk down for the night.

"Now, who needs a bite to eat?" she asked.

There was a loud *bang* and two *clunks* from the kitchen as Belle passed menus out among her unexpected but welcome guests. While she waited for decisions to be made, Belle leaned against the counter top and put her head down to speak in low tones to the girl with the Walkman, who occasionally nodded while passing her fingers across the right side of her mouth.

Corinna shook her head over the menu with much clucking and many facial expressions of disapproval.

"There isn't anything here I can eat!" she said at last, slapping the menu down on the table. "It's all either too fried or too full of calories..."

"You have to eat something," Keyes said in a motherly tone, in spite of himself.

"Oh, I think I'll just have a beer for now. I'd rather not screw up my diet unless I really have to."

Keyes made no further comment. Corinna weighed about one hundred pounds at her chubbiest, but Keyes had learned that one of the most futile things in this life was trying to convince certain women that they were not fat, and also as dangerous as hinting that they *were* fat; Corinna was one such woman. He set down his menu as well.

"I'm going to have a cheeseburger with the works, fries and gravy, and a large cherry coke!" he announced gleefully. Corinna gave him a look which suggested he had just dropped two levels on the food chain, a look he had often seen from his mother when he had made such dangerous dietary choices in her presence.

"Men will jump at just about any excuse to be sixteen again!" she groaned. Keyes grinned— he could find nothing in her statement to disagree with, not in his own case, anyway. Meanwhile, Belle had left the teenaged girl, and was making the rounds with order pad and pen.

"I'll have the banquet burger— rare, and make sure it's rare, 'cause I'm not afraid to send it back if it isn't..."

"Mashed potatoes or fries...?"

"Gimme the number seven, double order of sausage, hold the onions..."

"Comes with a roll..."

"Slice of pie, butternut-pecan ice cream, onion rings— *anddddd*... a root beer..."

"I want the biggest steak ya got, and burn the sonuvabitch..."

"HP Sauce or ketchup?"

"Scrambled eggs on brown toast..."

"Fish and chips with— no, wait, a minute, maybe the chili and toast would be better— oh, I don't know! Can you get back to me...?"

"Just a salad. Is there any Kraft Thousand Island dressing? I just love that..."

"Do you have light beer?" Corinna asked when Belle reached them. Belle shook her head and waved her hand in the direction of the cooler.

"Just what's there, sweetie, sorry."

"I guess I'll have a heavy one, then. Nothing else right now."

Keyes placed his burger-and-fries order rather boisterously, and Belle smiled in appreciation, patting him lightly on the cheek. "Good for you— looks like you're eating for both of you, anyway!"

Moanin' Joe approached them, on his way back from the general direction of the washrooms. "I'll have a toasted western on white, dash of cayenne, hold the fries." Belle nodded, scribbling on her pad as Joe continued, "Take long, ma'am? I could eat the hind end of a heifer."

"Depends on how moody the cook is, but our service is pretty quick under regular circumstances," Belle answered, then turned to the opening in the wall behind the counter which communicated with the kitchen.

"Are you cooking, Oswald?"

There was no sound from the kitchen, and the travellers fell silent, too, evidently as hungry as the cowboy.

"Oswald!"

Still there was silence.

"Are you sure there's anybody back there?" Joe asked. "Maybe he's stepped out."

"Tonight? Oswald's eccentric, but he's not crazy— the temperature's *still* dropping outside. He's back there all right— he's just yanking my chain. Oswald!"

This time there was a response, a sudden clamour of pots and pans being bashed and rattled, then bashed and rattled again. Belle turned back to her guests with a smile on her face.

"'Bout half an hour, folks!" she proclaimed, to murmurs of approval and a staccato burst of applause from Hawkwind. Then she began reading off items in a brisk voice to the man behind the window.

"Yah-hoo!" Hawkwind shouted, "Jah provides!"

Keyes shot a glance at Hawkwind, then leaned closer to Joe. "Is he all right?" he muttered.

Joe spread his hands. "Your guess is as good as mine, J.C. The kid's maybe one slice of bread short of a sandwich, but I don't see any harm in him..."

As Joe spoke, Corinna made a great show of ignoring him by studying her menu yet again, as if it was some modern Rosetta Stone which provided translation cues to the dialects spoken in the Blue Bayou. Then she tapped Keyes on the arm and passed him the menu.

"Look at this, Claude! Nobody knows how to spell 'Caesar' any more..."

Keyes took the dog-eared card and squinted: "You're right."
Joe peered over Keyes' shoulder.

"What's wrong with it?" he asked.

Keyes pointed to the offending word. "The 'e' and the 'a' in the diphthong are reversed— it's 'c-a-e,' not 'c-e-a'..."

"How about that? I think it looks okay."

"You would," Corinna said shortly. "Everybody in this country misspells it."

"Oh, don't be so fussy, Corinna," Keyes put in. "But, it is kind of sad— the last remnant of a great civilization, and nobody can even spell it right!" He studied his own copy of the menu for a moment, then pushed it across the counter to Corinna. "Look," he said, "this one's been corrected."

She looked: the "a" and the "e" had indeed been restored to a proper relationship with one another by means of a neat, serpentine editor's mark in red pencil.

"How comforting," she said.

Joe shook his head slowly from side to side, as if bemused by the whole discussion, then wandered off. Corinna pulled a paperback from her pocket— A Canadian Murder Mystery, Keyes could see proudly emblazoned across the back cover— and began to read.

Keyes turned to stare out the nearest window. This isn't so bad, after all, he thought. Shelter, food, interesting company— not necessarily the company he would have chosen for himself, but interesting nonetheless. There were certainly far worse places to be, and some more dangerous, in the middle of such wintery tumult; people were injured, even died in weather conditions like this, he reflected, and considered himself moderately lucky to be where he was. All in all, he was content to relax and enjoy the experience.

Soon the food began to arrive, and there was a stretch of comparative silence except for the distinctive sounds of a roomful of people eating. When everyone had finished, Belle began assigning quarters and handing out room keys with a cheery efficiency and brisk authority which allowed for no arguments.

"Young Jennet here can bunk down with Louise in number one," she said. "And you, honey," she said to Corinna, "I'll give you and your hubby the Honeymoon Suite— that's unit two." Keyes opened his mouth to lodge a formal protest against this sudden re-definition of his marital status, but Corinna stayed him with a sharp elbow to the ribs and a "don't make waves" look. "Joe and Evel Kneivel here will fit nicely into number three, and that leaves number four for you road-crew boys."

Then Belle turned her attention to the Cooks and the Bakers, in their skimpy, ice cream coloured clothes. "First off," she said, hauling a large cardboard box from under the counter and rummaging in it. "Here's a couple of coats for you girls, got left behind here about a month ago." She handed over to Darlene a cloth coat, simple enough in design, but a startling purple hue; the other was a many-coloured and down-filled ski jacket, which made Earlene resemble a large pigeon with pretensions of peacock-hood.

"Units five and six," Belle said, giving Darlene and Earlene each a key. "Listen, everybody— we'll be staying open pretty late tonight just in case any other refugees show up, so if anybody feels like coming back for a coffee or a beer, you're more than welcome; we can even bend the liquor laws a bit if we need to, given the circumstances."

There was a general murmur of thanks as coats were fastened and scarves tightened for the exodus to the motel rooms.

"I'll go get our stuff from the car, and meet you at the suite,"

Keyes said to Corinna, in what he supposed was a voice used by long-suffering husbands, rather hoping that Corinna would stand on her feminist principles and offer to help him with the bags.

"How thoughtful of you, dear," she said.

"Well, isn't he the old-fashioned gentleman!" Belle beamed approvingly. "You hold on to him, honey!"

"Oh, I will!" Corinna flashed an exaggeratedly carnivorous grin at Keyes, who frowned in return. "I will indeed."

19.

Keyes found a nightmare landscape of frozen frenzy immediately beyond the threshold of the Bayou. Although the Toyota was only a few dozen yards away, he began to wish for a lifeline with which to tether himself to the building. The wind was like a series of sharp slaps against his tender skin, and blowing strongly enough to keep him upright if he tripped. He fought with the car door, finally wrenched it open, and grabbed their overnight bags.

Had that big station wagon been there when they arrived? he wondered as he headed toward the motel units, now moving at double speed because of the piledriver wind at his back.

Corinna loudly applauded his pioneer spirit as he stepped inside. Keyes combined a small bow with a snow-dispersing shrug.

The Honeymoon Suite proved to be much like the rest of the establishment, unrelentingly clean, fully equipped with necessities and even a few small luxuries, and in disturbing taste. I suppose I could move into this motel if all else fails, Keyes thought. The walls were painted in what Belle had casually described as "hot pink," but looked more like faded blood to Keyes; the bedding continued the red motif in a slightly darker shade than the walls, with matching curtains on the single window.

"Kind of like stepping inside a huge wound," Keyes commented to Corinna.

"That's disgusting," Corinna said as she began pulling an unlikely number of toiletries and cosmetics from her bag. "Oh, damn it!"

"What?"

"No condoms!"

Keyes turned in surprise. Corinna was all but doubled over with laughter.

"I'm kidding! God, the look on your face! I've heard of gun-shy, but you're positively paranoid. Are you that afraid of women?"

"I am not afraid of women!" Keyes protested. "I just..."

"— never thought of me as one? Thanks, pal!"

"No, I—" Keyes glanced up from the depths of his hangdog blush to find her smiling again. "Lay off, Corinna. It's bad enough with this 'Mr. and Mrs. John Smith' routine."

"Oh, lighten up! It's fun. I know there's only one bed, but it's huge, and if you want we can string a blanket up between us, like in all those Rock Hudson and Doris Day movies— you'll be quite safe."

"You and I define 'safe' differently, then."

"Listen, Claude, I really did forget something: my nightgown. I hate sleeping in my clothes and I'll spare you the exquisite torment of my naked and unattainable self if you have a T-shirt or something you can lend me."

"How's this?" Keyes held out the top half of his flannel pyjamas, mauve with blue striping.

"You wear *pyjamas? Flannel* pyjamas?"

"My silk ones are being dry cleaned," Keyes replied with what was left of his dignity as he unpacked his own belongings. "But if you snore, I did bring my silk stockings— which I will use to stuff your nostrils."

"I do not snore!" Corinna announced as she swept into the bathroom, towel and toothbrush in hand.

It was Keyes' turn to grin.

20.

"Earlene and I are going to take *this* one," Darlene Cook announced outside the door of unit five. Earlene handed the key to number six to Fred.

"I'm very upset with you, George," Darlene continued, "about that scene with that boy in there. What will those people think of us?"

"But dear..." George said uncertainly, shivering in his madras shorts and flamingoed shirt.

"And you're no better, Fred Baker!" Earlene said.

Wrapping their borrowed coats about them, the two women made for the door of number five.

"Now just a damn minute," George said, starting after them.

The door slammed in his face.

"We should have been in the plane by now," Darlene said.

"Well, we aren't." Earlene looked bleakly about the unit's interior, which was pleasant enough, if ordinary, done up in various shades of pastel blue and earthy brown, with several paint-by-number landscapes on the walls. (One of these, however, was slightly out of place, although neither woman noticed; it was an amateurish rendition of an olive grove, among whose shadows sported several chubby and cheerful nymphs, and one rather exhausted-looking faun.) "We may as well settle in here— it's really not that bad."

"At least it's warm."

"What are we supposed to sleep in?" Earlene moaned.

"Our clothes, I guess."

"What time is it?" Earlene asked. "I've lost track."

Darlene glanced at her watch.

"Damn!" she said. "It's stopped. I guess it needs winding."

"Winding! You still have a wind-up watch!"

"I love this watch. My daddy gave it to me. Sometimes I forget to wind it."

Earlene went to the window and looked out. There was nothing to see but blackness and the occasional spray of snow against the glass.

"It doesn't matter anyway," she said. "If we can't go any place, it doesn't matter."

"Well, we can't, so we might as well go to bed."

"I'm not very tired," Earlene said.

"I'm not either, but what else is there to do?"

"I suppose we're lucky to be here, in a way."

"We could have run into a ditch in the middle of nowhere..." Darlene said.

"This is the outskirts of Stratford in February– it *is* the middle of nowhere."

They looked at each other. There were tears of frustration in Earlene's eyes. Darlene's jaw was set so firmly in anger that her lips were only a narrow red line across the lower part of her face.

They were big women, not especially tall, but bulky because of the inactivity of their lives and the junkiness of their diets. Because of their affluence, neither did housework. They always travelled by automobile, and never walked, except to the bottom of their gardens. They talked about joining aerobics classes or playing golf, but neither did. They ate "diet" lunches followed by rich desserts. They admitted that they were "round," but never thought of themselves as fat.

Darlene turned and looked at the double bed.

"Which side do you sleep on, Earlene?"

"Left. Fred is right-handed. Or he used to be. It's so long since he touched me that I can hardly remember."

"George still bites on my pillow now and then, but..."

They drew back the covers and crawled into the bed.

"God, it's lumpy," Earlene whined.

"And hard," Darlene added. "Some vacation. Good night, Earlene."

"Night-night, Darlene."

"Oh, shit, it's really *cold* in here!" George said miserably. His complaining was uncharacteristically justified. Unknown to Belle, the heating in unit six had broken down two hours earlier.

"Dark, too," Fred said, groping along the wall until he found a light switch. He flicked it several times, but the room remained wrapped in deep shadow. Fred swore mildly, then stepped carefully through the darkness to the table lamp beside the bed. He snapped it on, and the slight illumination of a forty watt bulb revealed a room decorated with dark grey stuccoed walls and light grey carpeting. Given warmth and more light, the effect would have been pleasant and soothing; as it was, unit six bore a passing resemblance to an unusually geometric ice age cave dwelling.

George and Fred groaned in unison.

"Well," George said, "we can't go griping about it right away—they'll think we're wimps or something!"

Fred nodded, then moved to the wall which they shared with unit five. There were muted sounds from the room beyond, the muffled sounds of their wives' talking and moving about.

"You're right," Fred said. "But in a while we can just go next door— they'll be missing us by then, right?"

"Right," George agreed. "But for the time being, we've got to keep from freezing our nuts off!"

Half an hour later, neither Earlene nor Darlene had managed to get to sleep.

"I'll never unwind if I can't get out of these britches," Darlene growled.

"My bra is killing me."

"Mine, too."

"I'm going to get undressed. You don't mind, do you?"

"Of course not. We'll both be more comfortable if we get out of our clothes."

They got out of the bed on opposite sides and, standing with their backs to it and to one another, they undressed. Then, with their large breasts swinging free and their large bottoms naked, they crawled again between the sheets.

"That's much better, isn't it?"

"It is... much."

From across the room, the frolicking nymphs peered out from their picture frame, and smiled broadly to themselves.

Fred and George sat uncomfortably on the floor of their room, grumbling and staring at the fire which George had kindled in a metal wastebasket. Both men were swathed in bedcovers, which hung on their out-of-shape bodies like poorly made coverings of animal skins. Fred was twitching nervously and clucking his tongue as George fed the flames with pages from the Bible he had found on the night table.

"God will understand," George said. "We have to keep warm, don't we?" But Fred kept seeing the conflagrations of eternal damnation in the tiny blaze. Finally, to divert his mind from the ripping sounds of sacrilege, he attempted to start a conversation.

"You know, George," he began, "there's one thing that's not too bad about this situation..."

"Yeah? What?"

"Well, it's kind of nice to be without the girls for a while... I mean, it gives us a chance to talk, you know, to bullshit like we used to."

George grunted, and with a sharp tug separated the Book of Ezekiel from the spine and tossed it into the basket. A deeper chill than that caused by the weather rippled up Fred's spine as each page flared up into a miniature demon, eagerly awaiting its chance to torment him.

"I saw on TV somewhere," Fred went on, "some guy who says that men should spend more time together, away from women, getting to know themselves as *real* men again—"

George glanced up from the tattered Bible in his hands; he had been trying to figure out whether the genuine simulated leather cover would burn or not. He frowned across the fire at his companion.

"Fred?"

"Yes, George?"

"What in hell are you talking about?"

Fred shrugged his bedspreaded shoulders, and silence fell over the room, which now felt even colder and gloomier to Fred, except for the small, ragged circle of light and warmth being generated by the Word of God.

"Are you chilly, Earlene?"

"I am. That woman said the heat worked in this room."

"Not very well, it doesn't."

"We could cuddle, like when we were kids."

"George never cuddles."

"Neither does Fred."

They cuddled.

"It is warmer, isn't it?" Darlene said.

"It is. It's a lot warmer."

"You'll go to sleep now, won't you, Earlene?"

"I think so..."

Fred was nodding drowsily, hypnotized by the wailing wind outside, when it abruptly stopped for a few moments. In the lacuna, he thought he heard the faint murmur of voices.

"George, listen."

"To what?"

"I can hear people talking."

"Well, I can't," George replied, noticing that he had almost reached the end of the fuel source; only the Book of Revelations remained. "Oh, wait..." he said, turning his head in the direction of their wives' room. "It's Darlene and Earlene yacking away."

"What do you suppose they're talking about?"

"How should I know? Swapping recipes, maybe. Women have pretty limited interests, Fred."

"I guess you're right, George."

"I am. Anyway, the fire'll be out soon, then we'll go next door."

Outside, the wind picked up again.

"Oh, Darlene!"

"Oh, Earlene!"

"Darlene... Darlene..."

"Earlene... Earlene... Earlene..."

"Oh, Darly!"

"Oh, baby!"

"Oh! Oh!"

"Oh! Oh! Oh!"

"Ooooooooooooooh!"

21.

"Looks like Ms. Belle has a flair for irony," Joe McKendricks remarked as he and Hawkwind settled into unit three.

Hawkwind frowned, and raised both thick eyebrows in question. Joe made a general gesture at their surroundings. "White walls, black carpet, black curtains, white bedspreads..." Hawkwind still looked confused. "Well, son, look at *us*: you're dressed all in white, I'm all in black..." Hawkwind shook his head, spread his hands in puzzlement, and slid cross-legged to the floor, where he began patting and searching among the various pockets of his suit. Finally, his mouth split in a huge grin of satisfaction as he produced a large reefer.

"You have fire, mon?" he said to Joe after a second search, for matches, was unsuccessful. Joe flipped a wooden match across the room. Hawkwind plucked it gracefully from the air, continuing the motion to strike the match against one of his many zippers, then to light the joint. After a few deep drags, he proffered the fat cigarette in Joe's direction. Joe shook his head.

"No thanks, son— makes me sleepy," he said, smiling at some old memory. Then, as he always did in new surroundings, Joe eased Ivy from the red plush lining of her case. Inevitably, the instrument's tuning had been affected by the recent exposure to various temperature changes. Joe strummed at the bronzed strings, brows knit and ear cocked for false notes. He executed several variations on a twelve-bar blues riff, followed by a short traditional Celtic ballad recently made popular again by Loreena McKennit, then twisted the tuning key on the B string, which snapped with a loud twang. Hawkwind's body twitched at the sound, then he leaned forward, his pale face slightly aglow with marijuana beatitude.

"Too tight, Toulouse?" he said.

"Hey, you're all right, son!" Joe laughed. "You know... now that I come to think of it, you remind me of my sister's boy, Mickey— 'cept of course he was blond, and maybe a foot taller than you... and I don't suppose you had to suffer through the great tragedy that he did..."

"Tragedy?"

"Yep, tragedy. Nobody knows quite how it came to be, all the doctors said they'd never seen nothing like it, but Mickey was born with this peculiar bone sticking out of his belly button; weirdest thing you ever saw: looked a lot like a slot-head screw..."

Hawkwind leaned forward even further, intrigued. Joe set Ivy to one side and rolled a cigarette as he continued.

"Anyway, he never had any pain or side-effects from this thing, but it caused him a lot of embarrassment as he grew up. He was teased by the other boys— you know how it is— and he got more and more obsessed by it when he became a teenager, worrying what girls would think of him... Up till then, he'd gone to church every day and prayed that one day this mutation or whatever it was would be healed, but on his thirteenth birthday he decided he had to do something drastic, something he'd been warned never, *ever* to do—"

"He gonna take the screw out himself!" Hawkwind interrupted excitedly.

"That's exactly it! One night, after everybody'd gone to bed, he sneaked into his Dad's tool shed and got a screwdriver, a bottle of rubbing alcohol, and a utility knife with a fresh blade, just in case. Then he climbed to the top of Batfowl Bluff outside of town, and, after praying for about an hour, got down to it. He swabbed his belly with the alcohol, and set the driver to the screw, and starting cranking the handle. Said later he felt a bit like one of them Japanese samurai, committing whaddayacallit—"

"Hara-kiri!" Hawkwind supplied.

Joe nodded. "But there wasn't a bit of pain. He said it tickled like the devil, and it was in there real tight, so he sat there for over half an hour, turning the screwdriver, and giggling. Then, that little bone just popped out onto the ground..."

"Was he okay?"

"Well, not exactly," Joe said gravely, turning to crush his cigarette out in an ashtray. He sat back and said nothing for a moment. "Mickey was so happy, he jumped to his feet and ran back down the hill, shouting and singing, doing little dances of joy— you can imagine the relief he must have felt, to be rid of this curse after all these years."

Hawkwind bobbed his head up and down emphatically.

"But then, just as he reached his front door, yelling for his parents and brothers and sisters to wake up, you know what happened?"

"What?"

"Well, son— his ass fell off..."

22.

"Unit one is Belle's best," Louise said to Jennet. The room had sky-blue walls, cloud-white shag carpeting, and two double beds.

"She must like you," Jennet said.

"I'm sure she does— I've overnighted here enough. But I kind

of think it's you she likes. You guys spent a long time talking in
there."

"Yeah," Jennet said. "She seemed nice."

"She is nice. She's had a rough go of it, but this place is doing
okay. It'll never make anybody rich, but Belle's never been much
interested in that, anyway. Well, me for a pee!"

While Louise was in the bathroom, Jennet unpacked her
rucksack, and noticed for the first time how ill-planned her flight
had been; the bag contained a mixed assortment of items thrown
hastily together in the half-light of morning: a book of poetry by
Arthur Rimbaud, three sets of underwear, a stuffed penguin
named Robertson, a pair of jeans (which, she now realized, she
had outgrown), several cassette tapes (The Doors, Blind Melon,
Me & My Uncle...), some T-shirts, a hairbrush, a random
selection of cosmetics and skin cleansers, a clinking handful of
loonies— and a letter, dog-eared and dirty from much handling.
She did not even remember packing the letter, but of course it
made sense that she would carry it with her, since it was the single
real treasure she had: the only communication Jennet had ever
received from her birth mother. "Dear Jennet (I know that's what
they call you, so I won't confuse you any further)..." it began, this
scrawled and incomplete attempt to explain why a very young and
confused woman had given her three-year-old daughter up for
adoption. The letter had been forwarded— probably by mistake—
from the adoption agency, and had no return address, just a
London, Ontario, postmark. Even the signature was illegible—
Bea, or Bonny, or perhaps Barb. Jennet had first read it four years
earlier, on her twelfth birthday, a year of great change for her, in
many ways; it was the year she had begun to menstruate, and the
year her stepfather's attitude toward her had shifted from bored
indifference to unwelcome and unpleasant attention.

Jennet made a small sound, somewhere between sob and chuckle. Louise was just coming out of the bathroom.

"Something the matter?" she asked.

"It's my birthday... I'm sixteen today," Jennet replied.

"Oh... happy birthday, kid. So... were you on your way to your grandparents' or somewhere, to celebrate?"

Jennet shook her head, then slowly began to tell Louise the story she had kept pent-up for so long— except for the brief snippets she had told Belle— in a voice tight with anger and bitterness. It was an intensely personal and sadly universal story, one told every day all over the world: young girl makes mistake, has child, has no money or power to raise child, gives up child to "good" home, child then suffers the misuse of trust and responsibility, child breaks free, or tries to...

"... I have this dream about a sleeping woman— I think she might be my real mother..." Jennet finished.

Louise was shaking her head. "So, are you trying to find her... your Mom?"

Jennet shrugged.

"I don't know. She might still be living around London somewhere. She might have moved. She might be dead. I'm not going back to the Cassells'; I didn't want to tell anybody about Burgess because it would break Barbara's heart, but nobody can make me go back and I don't have to explain anything!" Her tone was firm and challenging.

"Whoa!" Louise said, raising her palms. "*I'm* not going to try and send you back to that prick!"

Jennet smiled slightly, stood up, and went to the window.

"And, to top it all off," she said, "I have to turn sixteen on a night like this!"

"It was a night just like this that *I* left Buck Lamprey," Louise said in a musing tone.

"Buck who?" Jennet asked.

"Lamprey was his name. Mine, too, for six years. Everybody called him Buck... short for Ethelbert, if you can believe that."

"What happened?" Jennet asked.

"Well, it was a night like this... terrible storm. Blizzard... white-out... the whole enchilada-nordico." Louise looked out the window. "Buck was a mean sonuvabitch. Nobody liked him. Neither did I, I guess, but I wasn't much of a reader then and so I didn't know any of the stories about what happens to girls who get married just to get away from their parents or home towns, or whatever. And Buck didn't get really evil until a couple of years into the marriage."

"What did he do?"

"Just about everything. Not a week went by when I wasn't all bunged up. Black eyes, split lips... Anyway, we were out in a storm one night like this, just out to the hotel, but out, which was foolish. Buck drank too much, like he always did, and started slapping me around. The bartender told us to leave..."

Jennet's eyes went wide. "You mean he didn't help you, or call the cops or anything?"

Louise laughed, or made a bruised noise that was something like Jennet's earlier attempt at a laugh.

"Times were a bit different, kid. Nobody thought it was proper to interfere in a family's business. Buck was out of money anyway. But when we got to the car, he couldn't get it started. The thing was a big old Cutlass Supreme, cranky at the best of times. He swore at it, and then, when it was finally running, he couldn't get the windshield wipers to work... all iced up. So he gave me a scraper and told me to get out and clean off the windshield."

"Wow— he *was* a sonuvabitch!"

"That's what I said. Big windshield on a Cutlass Supreme, too, but I grew up on a farm and knew all about disagreeable work. When I tried to get back in the car Buck started bad-mouthing me, telling me to stay out of his car."

"He wouldn't let you in the car?" Jennet said, outraged. She still maintained a sort of naive faith that, as terrible as her experiences with Burgess Cassell had been, men like him were rare. (She hadn't had much trouble dealing with the hormonally-challenged teenaged boys of her acquaintance, even the one who had licked her hand at a party in some sort of demonstration, she supposed, of romantic interest; she had slapped the boy and washed the hand thoroughly, and that had been that.)

"Nope, not until I'd cleaned off the back window. I slammed the door and went around to the back of the car. The wind was blowing a gale and you could hardly see. A Cutlass is a big car, long body, big trunk..."

Jennet shifted impatiently. Cars were of no particular interest to her, especially old cars made south of the border in times of great decadence.

"I stood out there, freezing my ass," Louise said. "I could imagine Buck inside mumbling to himself about what a shitty wife I was, that I never did any work, that I couldn't cook, that I was a bad lay..."

Louise stopped to pull her dark undershirt off over her impressive hair, to reveal an even more impressive torso which made Jennet's jaw drop— she had never seen a woman's body like Louise De Wetering's, and couldn't help staring. While obviously female, it was more like some of the boys' bodies she had observed in the gym at school, specifically those who worked out regularly on weights; even Louise's breasts were like another pair of elegantly sculptured muscles which rippled every time she moved. Jennet could tell that there wasn't an ounce of fat on her roommate, not one square inch of flesh that hadn't been planned and worked for. Louise was six feet tall. The whole effect stunned the girl. Then Jennet caught sight of her own open-mouthed expression in the bureau mirror, and turned her head abruptly, her facial skin crimsoning.

"Sorry, I..." she mumbled.

Louise laughed loudly, held her right arm up in a classic body builder's pose, and flexed. Muscles bobbed and tensed in a pirouette of physical perfection.

"Don't worry about it, pal," she said. "You don't work as hard as I have to get a shape like this without expecting somebody to stare once in a while."

Jennet looked again, as Louise removed her uniform pants, revealing long, hard legs which matched the rest of her. The girl found herself simultaneously fascinated and a bit revolted by the sight, but was warming to Louise herself, who continued speaking while pulling on jeans and a bulky red turtleneck sweater.

"Anyway, there I was, standing behind that fucking Cutlass, middle of the night, shivering my tits off, holding onto that snow scraper as if it was an axe... it's a good thing it wasn't an axe, or I might've done some serious pruning on Buck Lamprey. Instead, I dropped the scraper, turned around, and walked away."

"So, what happened to Buck?"

"Who cares? He was so stupid he might still be there waiting for me, for all I know. But I promised myself as I trudged through that blizzard that I wouldn't ever be a victim again. Once I got settled, I started working out and, well, you just saw the result. Nobody touches me if I don't want to be touched... not more than once, anyway!"

"But do you still, I mean... you know, like men? Or are you a— oh, geez, I'm sorry..." Jennet trailed off, blushing, more deeply this time. Louise's smile became broader as she leaned across the bed and patted Jennet's scarlet cheek gently.

"No, I'm not a lesbian, sweetie." The corners of Louise's mouth twisted into a wicked burlesque of sexual enticement. "But I *do* insist on being on top!"

23.

Cassell had become so nervous over having recognized his present location that he had just about made up his mind to give up on Jennet, back the car out of this place and head back to Cornerpost, weather be damned; he was also drunk enough that he was not completely capable of making sensible decisions. Burgess Cassell had never been given to deep introspection anyway, and he was unaware of how confused his judgement became under the influence of gin and certain types of teenaged girls, no matter the weight of historical evidence supporting these traits.

The decision to remain or flee was, however, taken out of his hands when he discovered that he was out of gas. He immediately began cursing Bibsy's incompetence, although it was Cassell himself who had forgotten to fill the tank before barreling off in pursuit of his stepdaughter.

"I'll freeze out here..." he mumbled to the empty gin bottle.

Cassell made a simian growl deep in his throat, and waited. Some time before, he had seen the door of the Blue Bayou open and disgorge various groups of people. He hadn't been able to make out Jennet among them, but she had to be there somewhere. Cassell had hunkered down in his seat until he was sure that everyone had entered rooms in the guest facility across the parking lot.

This is good, he thought. Soon they would all be settled in for the night, and he could slip inside, warm up a bit, get some gasoline... and find out what was going on with Jennet from the proprietor, what room she was in. And another drink...

It seemed to Cassell that he waited in the frigid limbo for forty days and forty nights.

24.

"Geez, this is a pretty nice room," Gordy said as he conscientiously wiped the snow from his boots on the corrugated rubber mat inside the door of number four.

"It's painted prison-fucking-green, Gordy," Peavine answered in a disagreeable tone. "There's a velvet-fucking-Elvis painting on the wall, Gordy! There's no cable-fucking-TV, Gordy! This is a cell! It is no way pretty-fucking-nice! Jee-zus, man!" Peavine threw himself down on the larger of the two beds— this unit had a king-sized model, and a smaller, child-sized one— his own boots dripping snow and mud onto the twining-leaf patterned bedspread.

"Okay, Peavine... whatever you say," Gordy mumbled. It had not escaped him that his partner had knocked back half a dozen bottles of beer in the brief time they had been inside the Blue Bayou's diner, and that Peavine was now beginning to suck on a pint of cheap rye which had magically appeared from the inside pocket of his parka, although liquor was, of course, forbidden on the job. With each drink, Gordy was aware of Peavine's surliness quotient increasing, although there were no outward signs of drunkenness; Choate was one of those men whom liquor affected mainly in the head, and not for the better.

Gordy sat down on the edge of the small bed gingerly, unwilling to disturb the tight and carefully-creased covers. He decided that conversation might not be the wisest thing, given Peavine's mood. He pulled a small New Testament from his pocket, and opened it to where he had last been reading. Gordy Doig was not a particularly religious man, but Midge in the office was a church-going girl, and he hoped, if he ever got his courage up, to know enough about the Bible to steer their conversation to something other than the weather. Unconsciously he began reading aloud in a hushed whisper of reverence induced more by the incomprehensible mysticism of the material than by piety:

"And there appeared a great wonder in heaven... a woman clothed with the sun and the moon under her feet... and upon her head a crown of twelve stars—"

"Jesus Christ, Gordy!" Peavine said loudly, lurching to his feet. "If you're gonna go holy roller on me, I'm taking a walk!"

"A walk? In this? But Peavine..."

Peavine was not listening to Gordy. His eyes glazed over. He took another long swig of rye. He was seeing the long legs of the redheaded bus driver, and the untidy waves of blonde hair on the little babe she was bunking with... He was seeing them removing their travel clothes, maybe having a shower together, maybe scrubbing each other's backs, or scrubbing each other's—

He shook his head sharply. Why bother imagining things when the real items were so close? What were windows for, anyway? It might not be too bad a night, after all, Peavine thought, and that Belle wasn't too bad herself, for an older broad. He zipped his parka, then pulled on his hat and gloves. He stepped outside, bracing himself against a sudden rush of wind, then turned right and headed down the sidewalk to the end of the block of units. Behind the building the snow was nearly waist-deep, and Peavine began plowing his way through it toward the opposite end, toward the soft patch of light emanating from unit number one.

25.

Belle placed the last of the miscellaneous cups and bottles into a plastic bus bin, then trudged slowly to the dishwasher, the smile almost, but not quite, gone from her face, and with less of a spring in her step now that her guests had departed. She was very tired, but had always believed that anyone in the service industry should not burden the customers with his or her own weariness or troubles. This attitude, while sometimes hard on Belle's equanimity, had made the Blue Bayou popular. She and Oswald had stayed in business when many other more fashionable and elegant establishments had gone under.

"Oswald!" she called through the access window.

Rat-a-tat, ka-thump, clang!

"Oh, stuff the percussion, will you? I'm getting a headache! I think you better go down to the cellar and check our inventory on coffee and breakfast stuff. We don't know how long we might have to feed this lot."

There was no reply from Oswald, either in Latin or lid-banging, but Belle heard his footsteps descending the cellar stairs. Now that she was alone, she allowed the suppressed exhaustion which had been building inside her to surface, as she went to her stool behind the cash register and sat, then pulled open a drawer beneath the counter. Among various order pads and receipt books was a small stack of pale green envelopes, bound with twine. A fine mist formed over her eyes as she stared at the letters: she had written them regularly over the years, but stopped mailing them after the first ones had been returned from the adoption agency which had been entrusted with her daughter; her baby daughter, the child she had not seen in so very long... Belle pulled a tissue from her apron and dabbed at her eyes, then tugged a photograph from the pile of envelopes, the single Polaroid which she had been sent of the child: a three-year-old with big eyes, and a big smile. Belle sobbed aloud as she recalled her conversation with the girl named Jennet.

The familiar scrape of the front door opening and the wind beyond shattered Belle's reverie. She turned to see a man standing there uncertainly, shivering and shaking the snow from his shoulders. At first she thought it was one of the others returning, but soon realized that this was a fresh refugee, and an intoxicated one. He was swaying and glancing furtively around the room. When his gaze landed on her, it immediately made her wary, for no reason she could name other than an obvious one: she had been robbed once, years before, under similar circumstances—

alone with a drunk stranger, late at night, during inclement weather. She thought of her little gun, then shook her head at her own paranoia; this fellow was only another lost soul seeking a bit of warmth and comfort on a miserable night.

"Come on in," she said. "Have a seat. Can I get you something?"

Cassell still did not speak, but shambled forward until he was only a foot or so from Belle, who was standing beside the cash register. At this distance, Belle saw a look in the man's eyes which was hunted and predatory at the same time. It was a wild and disoriented look which disturbed her all over again. With one hand she slid open the cash drawer in order to give her quick access to her weapon.

"I'm looking for somebody," Cassell said at last. "A girl, blonde, about sixteen... she shouldn't be out alone... she needs me..."

Belle gave a small involuntary gasp. It was him, the man Jennet had told her about. The kid had not wanted to talk at first, but Belle had been concerned enough about a girl her age travelling alone that she had been able to fish out of her a few sparse facts: Jennet's age, where she was from, and that she was running away from home, specifically from the unwanted attentions of her stepfather.

"There's no one like that here!" Belle snapped, losing her self-control. Hate and disgust rose in her at this creature who had abused his most sacred responsibilities. Belle had been a child herself, no older than Jennet, when she had given birth; she had trusted the system to see that her baby would have a chance at the good life which Belle couldn't give her, as had Jennet's own natural mother, no doubt... and *this* was the result—

"Don't lie to me, you bitch!" Cassell rumbled. "I saw her... I'll find her!"

There was a brief but intense silence as the two glared at one another, broken softly by the sound of footsteps in the kitchen behind them.

26.

It had been a long time since Jennet had guffawed as loudly as she did with Louise De Wetering. The wind outside laughed along with them, and when she and Louise stopped to catch a breath, so did the wind. There was a sharp, distant *crack*, and Jennet, although she could not tell from what direction the sound came, automatically turned toward the window, and looked right into the broad, leering face of Peavine Choate.

Although not ordinarily easily intimidated, Jennet was as susceptible to the panic of a sudden shock as the next person—unless the next person was Louise De Wetering. While Jennet scuttled backward away from the window, clutching a pillow to her half-naked body, Louise leapt immediately forward, whipping the towel from her wet hair and winding it around her right hand and forearm. She smashed the protected fist through the thin glass and popped Peavine squarely on the nose, hard enough to draw blood.

"Get the fuck out of here!" she bellowed. Peavine obeyed, staggering backward. He disappeared from view in the swirling snow.

"You okay?" Louise asked Jennet, who nodded, recovering

her composure. Louise stood with her hands on her hips, shaking her red mane at the broken window. "Damn that asshole! It's going to get pretty cold in here."

"Maybe we should go take *his* room," Jennet suggested with a small smile.

"Maybe we will!" Louise agreed. "But for now let's just try and plug up the hole..."

Which they did, with towels and extra blankets, giggling, as if both were twelve years old and labouring to hide the evidence of a girlish prank from the disapproving eyes of an authoritarian camp counsellor.

27.

When she returned from the bathroom a few minutes later, Corinna went straight to a mirror on the wall opposite the bed. It was a small mirror, too small to be considered a picturesque appendage to the bed itself. Its frame was decorated with exotic beer-bottle tops, disks of metal from remote provinces and foreign states: Moosehead, Rainer, Imperator, Stella Artois...

On her way to the mirror she stripped off her pullover, and began to arrange her hair, then to rearrange it. Keyes watched her for a moment, admiring her total lack of embarrassment and the slender beauty of her back and shoulders. Her breasts, he had noticed as she passed him, were full and shapely, seeming to require the black bra that contained them more for cover than support. They were lovely breasts, he thought, not that he hadn't made this observation before. He was beginning to wonder whether he would get through the night without requesting the return of his pyjama shirt.

"Do you have a book I can borrow?" Keyes asked, seeking distraction where he could find it. "I accidentally brought one I've already read, and it wasn't that hot the first time."

Corinna nodded without taking her eyes from her attentions to her own face, and pointed to her kit on the bed. "Not the murder mystery— I'm still reading it... the other one."

"Is the mystery any good?" Keyes asked as he rummaged through the bag. He read detective fiction sporadically, if it had been recommended as exceptional or out of the ordinary.

"It's shit!" Corinna pronounced. "And it shouldn't be!"

"Well... nothing *should* be shit, Corinna. Except of course shit itself."

"That's not what I mean. I know the author. We published her first book, short stories, a few years ago, and it was good. Flawed, sure, but I felt if she kept going in the same direction she'd really be somebody. Then she started writing these formula things, and all that talent and potential just dried up!"

"Everybody has to eat..." Keyes said. And live somewhere, he thought. And be able to buy their own driveways.

"That's what *I* said at first. I figured she was doing this detective series to buy her time to develop her other work. But she just gave up on it; said it was too hard or some such garbage. Of course it's hard— it's supposed to be! You know how I feel about sell-outs..."

I do indeed, Keyes thought. He found a second paperback, a thick novel with a lurid black and scarlet cover. The jacket copy informed him that he was about to be thrilled and chilled by vampires terrorizing the Shaw Festival in Niagara Falls. After about half an hour, he gave up on the tale. It was well written enough, but there was simply too much bloodletting and off-centre sex for his current mood.

"I think I'm going to take Belle up on her offer and go back to the diner for some coffee," he said, shrugging into his greatcoat as he peered out the window. "The lights are still on over there."

"*I'm* going to sleep," Corinna replied, now beneath the bedcovers, pillows propping her up as she continued with her own book. "I'm knackered."

"See you later, then," Keyes said over his shoulder as he closed the door behind him. The roaring of wind and snow around the building paused for a moment, as if gathering strength, and he heard a door slam to his right. Keyes turned his head to see Joe McKendricks exiting number three, and waited for him. In spite of the weather, Joe ambled along at his own deliberate pace, a man in complete control of his own life, a man for whom the rest of the world could damn well wait until he got to it. Keyes smiled— this was the sort of man he could not help but admire.

"Thought I might get a drink," Joe said as he reached Keyes. "You know, that kid is as weird as a waltzing wildebeest!"

"Hawkwind?" Keyes inquired as they headed through the bitter chill toward the main building.

Joe nodded. "The same."

They were the only ones from the group to return, so far, but music rattled from the juke box, a tune Keyes liked in spite of himself.

You let me get away with Molly and Loretta,
You turned a blind eye to Carly and Louise;
You never said a word about Anna-Lee or Greta,
But then you cut me off at Denise.

Keyes glanced at the brown bottles of Canadian beer newly lined up on the shelf below the pies in the refrigerated display case behind the counter, but he wasn't thirsty. Even coffee, considering the amount he had drunk earlier, was unattractive to him. Keyes realized that he had really wanted to put some distance between himself and Corinna's suddenly seductive presence. He was, he admitted, unsettled by the move from Toronto and its unforeseen complications, by the imminent completion of his new book, by worries about his mother's health, by the blizzard itself. The prospect, no matter how slim, of romantic involvement with Corinna was simply too weird for him right now. Then Corinna had unnerved him even further with her foreshadowing rant about writers with no literary integrity. She might, he admitted, be extremely understanding if Keyes were forced to accept Cosmodemonic's offer. And the snow might all melt away in the next hour, too.

At a little table behind the cash register Belle sat with her back to the two men. She was poring over a big book of some sort, an accounts ledger, Keyes supposed, and entirely caught up in whatever she was doing to it.

Keyes and Joe slid into a booth near the front window. The storm raged on outside. There were drifts as tall as Joe, and the vehicles in the parking lot were completely covered, burial mounds in Valhalla.

"Snow, which is death..." said Moanin' Joe as he looked out into the night. "So you're a writer, eh? You said you're moving here?" he asked.

"Moving back, in a way... I used to work at the Theatre."

Joe's eyes widened.

"You aren't Will Shakespeare risen from the dead, are you, J.C.?"

Keyes grinned. "No, and I'm not Gilbert and Sullivan, either."

"Who?" Joe said.

"Never mind." Keyes was having trouble figuring Joe out. The man wasn't quite the simple rustic troubadour he had appeared to be at first.

"You writers travel a lot, don't you?" Joe asked.

"Some do, some don't— it's not a requirement."

"Hmmm. Do you know Stignano?"

Keyes shook his head warily.

"Place in Calabria I did a gig." The *a*'s in Calabria were flat and entirely un-Italian, but there was no hint of doubt in Joe's voice as he spoke.

"Italy?" Keyes' astonishment was apparent.

"Of course in Italy. You don't know any other Calabrias, do you?"

"You're not going to tell me you played Calabria!"

"Yes, I am."

"Country songs?"

"More western than country. Those Calabrese love us western stars."

"First I've heard of that particular cultural crossover!"

"Pay attention, J.C. This is a true story."

Keyes had an instinctive feeling that what he was about to hear had very little of the truth in it.

"I was a big success in Stignano," Joe continued. "People loved me... and they couldn't understand a word of English, most of them. I sang a dozen encores, maybe two dozen..." He paused as if recalling the glories of old Calabria. "The mayor invited me to his house for dinner the next day... fellow named Don Ilario. The whole family was at the table... three generations of them."

"Something you don't see much of in North America these days," Keyes commented.

The cowboy frowned at the interruption, then went on: "Lots of wine to drink and noodles to eat, or maybe they weren't noodles exactly. My dad would have said they were noodles. The biggest bowl of noodles I ever saw."

"Pasta, the Italians call it," Keyes said helpfully.

Joe began to chuckle, and shake his head from side to side.

"What is it?"

"Oh, I just remembered something funny about that meal."

"Funny?" Keyes said.

"Yeah, funny. I don't know how it happened, but right in the middle of the meal, one of the babies fell into the noodles... the pasta, I mean."

Keyes gasped. "Fell in!"

"That's right. Little kid, naked as a jaybird. He went right into the... pasta."

"He could have drowned," Keyes said, "or suffocated..."

"Not the way he went in... bottom first. And he wasn't there long. He howled like a scalded cat."

"Of course he did, poor guy. Was he hurt?" Keyes had a certain fondness for babies— those belonging to other people, that is.

"Oh, no. His mom was right there, but she had another kid and she'd turned away a minute to see to her, and that's when the little fella flopped in the pasta. They put some olive oil on his butt after they hauled him out, just in case."

Keyes was relieved that the baby hadn't been injured. "What a waste of pasta!" he said, being a man who enjoyed his spaghetti, fettucini, and rigatoni.

Joe grinned. "Oh, they didn't waste it. Those Calabrese are

thrifty people. Once they got the baby out, the bowl went on around the table. I was just glad I already had *my* noodles."

Keyes had a sour thought, then, and could not resist asking the question: "Why were you so glad to have yours already? The baby didn't... *do* anything in the pasta, did it?"

Joe's grin widened then, as if he were an angler and Keyes the trout who has taken his line.

"Why, J.C., what an unpleasant idea! These were fastidious folks— you could eat off their floors! I just personally don't care for the taste of baby powder with my noodles."

Keyes gave Joe a solemn and pained look.

"I can't believe I sat still for that," Keyes said grimly.

"True story," said Moanin' Joe. "I need me a beer." He turned in his seat. "Belle! Could I get a beer when you got a second?" Joe turned back to Keyes, who was flipping the selector knob on the juke box unit. The two men sat in comfortable silence for a while, then Joe said:

"What're they doin'? Brewin' that beer? I'll be back in a minute, J.C."

Keyes nodded distractedly— he was listening to a song which, as near as he could tell, concerned a woman attempting to decide between a drunken lover and a convict husband; there was also mention of a German Shepherd, but Keyes could not sort out whether this part of the story concerned man's best friend or Prussian animal husbandry. He read through the artists' names— a lot of Hank Williams, Loretta Lynn, some Garth Brooks, Bruce Aubrey, Johnny Cash— then fished in his pocket for a quarter. He punched in a couple of songs whose titles caught his fancy, and was just about to take the plunge and find out if Sneezy Waters' music was as good as his name, when he was interrupted by Moanin' Joe.

"Keyes, c'mere— I think we might have a small hostess problem..."

A loud fanfare of fiddles and harmonicas churned from the juke box as Keyes looked to see McKendricks bent over Belle, who had not moved in the last ten minutes.

"Hostess problem?" Keyes said as he joined them. "What kind of a problem is that?"

McKendricks pointed a skeletal finger. "When your hostess is dead from a gunshot wound, I reckon it's a problem..."

There was indeed such a wound in Belle's breast, disfiguring the crispness of her otherwise immaculate blue uniform. There was very little blood, but some of what there was had trickled over Belle's nametag, effacing all of the letters but for the large and bold "B." Keyes drew in a sharp breath, felt himself go cold and stiff. He averted his eyes quickly, and saw that one of Belle's shoes had slipped from her foot. The shoe was blue, as well. Keyes began to tremble slightly. He had only seen violent death once before, and in this same town. It was no easier to endure now than it had been then.

"Are you sure...?" Keyes asked shakily.

"I'm sure. There's no pulse... and I'm sorry to say I've seen this kind of wound before. It's fatal." Then, in a softer growl than usual, McKendricks said, "Easy, friend," and placed an open bottle of beer in Keyes' hand. Keyes stared at the image on the label, a black-sailed schooner on a tempest-tossed sea...

"Police," was all Keyes could think of to say. "But Belle said the phones were out of order."

Moanin' Joe nodded. There was a telephone beside the cash register, but he set the receiver down after he had picked it up and listened.

"Still nothin'. Try that pay phone over by the door."

Keyes obeyed, but slowly, as he tried to adjust himself to this sudden new and unpleasant situation, to thrust aside by force of will the dark wooliness occluding his thinking.

The pay phone, too, was dead. As dead as Belle...

The song on the juke box came to a raucous conclusion, and in the silence a banging sound behind them caused both men to snap to attention, and Keyes' head cleared somewhat. He hurried through the connecting open doorway to the kitchen. The back door was open a small crack, admitting slivers of snow. It slammed shut, then blew open again a few inches, stopped by a cast iron cooking pot on the floor. The pot must have fallen from its hook on the wall, and prevented the door from opening all the way. It was also the source of the sound which had surprised them— they had not heard it earlier because of the juke box.

Melting puddles on the red-tiled floor indicated that the door had been behaving in this fashion for some time. Some of the puddles, to Keyes' eyes, were foot-shaped. He shoved the pot aside with his foot, then braced himself and went outside. It was cold and wild, and Keyes reconnoitred as much as he was able without straying too far from the reassuring light of the building, dim and distant though it seemed on occasions when the drifting became intense. After a few freezing seconds, he gave up and stumbled back into the kitchen. He looked half man and half sugar-plum fairy. His windward side was plastered with snow; one eye was closed by it, and one ear too, painfully. There was snow down his shirt collar, up his trouser legs, and, mysteriously, in his underwear.

"Jesus!" he muttered, shaking himself like a dog.

Keyes turned to close the door at his back. This proved to be no easy matter. In the moments he had been outside, the storm had driven several bushels of the white stuff into the kitchen and dumped it on the floor. He kicked and pawed at the accumulation, until he had cleared a space and finally succeeded in shutting out the winter.

"Where's Joe?" He asked himself, wondering if the cowboy had followed him outside. Even as he said it, something told him that this was not the case.

He crossed the kitchen back into the restaurant. Joe was where he had left him, standing beside the cash register. Belle's body, however, had disappeared beneath an avalanche of paper and cloth— beer posters from the back of the bar, a large calendar with photographs of vintage railway engines on it, Christmas cards, valentines, and post cards. Predominant among her shrouding was a large Canadian flag, frayed along the edges.

"What happened?" Keyes asked.

"Wind," Joe said. "Didn't your mama teach you to close the door behind you when you went outside?"

"I couldn't find anybody."

"No, you wouldn't— not in this weather. See anything?"

"Footprints on the kitchen floor... a few of them..."

"No hope of tracking anybody outside in this mess. You're lucky you got back yourself." Joe raised his hand. There was a bottle of rye in it. "You look like you could use a snort of this."

The snow and ice that clung to Keyes was melting in the warm room. Icy rivulets ran down his person both inside and outside his clothes. His teeth began to chatter like very un-Canadian castanets.

"I... I agree..." he stammered between unclenchable teeth.

Joe reached across the counter and found a glass beneath it somewhere. He seemed to know where to find the glass, as if he had served time as a bartender in one place or another. He poured an ample tot for the shaking Keyes.

"A wee dram," Joe murmured in a not particularly country-and-western way.

Keyes took the glass, and drank. His shuddering slowed immediately. He shook his head and drank again, a sip the second time.

"You know, J.C., this makes me think of the death of Berlioz," Joe said.

Keyes almost choked on the sip of whiskey in his throat.

"What?" he gasped.

"Berlioz." The cowboy pronounced it to rhyme with Cheerios. "A Frenchman..."

"I know who he is."

"*Symphonie Fantastique...*" Again the words became entirely North American, as local as breakfast cereal even if there was no rhyme to what he said. "*The Trojans...*"

"I said I *know* who he is. But..."

"Well, he died like that."

Keyes searched his memory but could find nothing there about the death of Hector Berlioz.

"Don't you think we ought to..." He nodded toward the heap of trash which covered Belle's body.

"In a minute," Joe said. "She's not going far, and you need time to let that rye work into you far enough to keep you from catching the grippe."

"And in that time you're going to tell me about the death of Berlioz?"

"Doesn't seem like a bad idea, does it?"

Keyes backed away to a chair, sat down, and sipped again from his glass.

"I guess not," Keyes admitted.

"Well," Joe began in a deliberate tone that suggested the story might be a long one, "it seems that when Berlioz was an old man, the people in his home town decided to invite him back to show their appreciation..."

Already Keyes was into it. "First time, I'd bet."

"And you'd win. The folks in a man's home town are always the last to admit that the punk kid they all hated for being smarter than they were had amounted to something."

"Where was this town?"

Joe shook his head. "Can't remember the name of it." He helped himself to another whiskey. "Anyways, they had this big dinner party in the town hall for the native son. Everybody in town who was anybody— the mayor, the town council, the doctors, lawyers, preachers..."

"Priests, more likely," Keyes corrected.

"Priests preach, don't they? Anyhow, all the town fathers and a lot of the town mamas too. A great long table with a hundred candles on it, people up and down both sides of it, and poor old Berlioz smack in the middle in a special chair, like a throne. They'd hung a lot of flags and stuff up behind him to mark the place. I guess he was kind of a skinny little guy, and old..."

"Pick up the pace, Joe."

"There were speeches and toasts... the French are big on toasts..."

"Because they have good wine— a toast won't work without good wine."

Joe grinned. "You're full of it, J.C.... you know that?"

"You're not the first to tell me so. Go on."

"Well, in the middle of all this toasting and speechifying, a storm came up... did I say this was up in the mountains?"

Keyes nodded.

"You know how mountain storms can be... all thunder and

lightning and wind. It blew and rattled and shook until one of the windows in the town hall popped open. Wind and rain whooshed into the banquet hall, blew all the candles out, blew all the skirts up and all the hats off... There was a lot of shouting and milling around in the dark until somebody got the window secured and somebody else got some candles re-lit. When things calmed down, they remembered the guest of honour, but he was nowhere to be seen."

Keyes glanced at the forlorn heap of litter that covered poor Belle's remains. Joe noted the direction of Keyes' look, and nodded sagely.

"That's right. The flags had blown down and Berlioz was lying under a pile of red, white, and blue bunting, just like Belle over there under the maple leaf."

"And he was dead?"

"By the time they dug him out, he was. He was old, as I said. I guess the shock of it got him."

"Who told you that story, Joe?"

"You doubtin' me?"

"Not exactly, but I'm an opera fan, and Berlioz wrote lots of operas—"

"I said that. *The Trojans...*"

"— and I've never heard this story."

"Well, I got it from a fiddle player named Wilf Hartley. We worked together in a bar called Empty Saddles out in Saskatchewan. He used to play in big orchestras— symphonies and that sort of thing, but when he had his druthers, he played in country bands."

"He could drink on the job."

Joe nodded philosophically. "That may have had something to do with it. Wilf enjoyed his jar."

They sat quietly for a minute, looking at the flag and the body it partially covered.

"Let's get her out of there, Joe," Keyes said at last.

Joe hesitated. He looked over his shoulder at the door, then out a window at the storm.

"Well, there's nobody around," he said. "But... you know, the police don't take kindly to anybody moving things at the scene of the crime."

"As you say, there's nobody around, and we can't just leave her like that, can we?"

"No, I guess it wouldn't be decent. It's just that I've had troubles with the fuzz in the past..."

The *fuzz?* Keyes thought. "Okay, I'll tell the cops *I* moved her. Come on."

They went to Belle's body, although Joe lagged behind, as if he didn't want to do what he knew he would be required to do. Keyes pulled aside the flag. The woman beneath it looked much younger than he had thought upon first meeting her.

"Take her feet, Joe."

Together they lifted the corpse. It was easy to do. Belle was a small woman; pitifully small, Keyes thought.

"What'll we do with her?" Joe asked. He did not look happy.

Keyes glanced around the room. The benches in the booths were narrow and the tables short. None of them would accommodate Belle, or what was left of her, tiny though she was.

"The counter," Keyes said. "We'll put her on the counter."

Joe backed in that direction. Keyes swung about.

"One for the money," Joe chanted, "and two for the show."

On "show" they swung their burden up and settled it between the soda taps and the cash register. Joe plucked at Belle's skimpy skirt, pulling it down to cover her knees.

"Small wound," Joe observed. ".22, or something like that."

"In this case," Keyes said grimly, "size doesn't really matter, does it?"

Keyes went back to the heap of trash in the midst of which Belle had lain. He noticed her order pad, a tube of lipstick, and a thin packet of envelopes held together with binder twine. Out of tidy habit, he scooped these items up and dropped them into his jacket pocket, then gathered the folds of the red and white flag. He returned to Joe, and the two men covered the corpse with the flag. The maple leaf was draped across Belle's mid-section like a funeral wreath.

"Like a burial at sea," Keyes commented, remembering a film he had seen, or rather a genre of films in which nautical burials frequently occurred.

"Except for the lack of water, at least any that isn't frozen solid," Joe said. "How about another snort of some other liquid?"

Keyes shook his head, but realized that he did want a drink, after all.

"A sip," he said.

Joe poured. While shorter than the last drink he had served Keyes, it was nonetheless more than a sip.

"Thanks," Keyes said, raising the glass toward his lips. He stopped it before it got there, so abruptly that he splashed whiskey down the front of his shirt.

"Wait a minute!" he said. "Whatever happened to Oswald?"

28.

Joe frowned. "The elusive Oswald— a good question."

"I didn't see him in the kitchen," Keyes said, setting his glass on the counter near Belle's bunting-covered right foot.

Joe put his glass beside the same foot, and the bottle beside that.

"Maybe we should take another gander in there."

Keyes was already on his way.

He had not noticed before how small the space was— to call it a kitchen was to glorify it; galley would have been a better term. Keyes had known closets bigger than the Blue Bayou's kitchen, had in fact lived in smaller closets, on tour, during his acting days.

He heard Joe somewhere behind him, fumbling among cooking utensils. Then there was a tremendous clatter, and Keyes whirled to see Joe attempting a paradiddle with wooden spoons on the array of long-handled pots that dangled from the ceiling.

"Oswald!" the cowboy bellowed. There was no reply.

Keyes bent to look under a counter, opened the refrigerator, threw open cupboards, even checked inside the large oven.

"No place a man could hide," he said, "unless he was of the vertically-challenged persuasion."

"What're those?" Joe asked, pointing at a narrow stack of shelves beside the stove. "Cookbooks?"

There were tins of tomato, beans, tuna fish, peaches, pineapples, and sardines. Somehow Keyes doubted that Oswald required recipe books to prepare what was served at the Blue Bayou. Haute cuisine was beyond the capabilities of the establishment, and beyond its pretensions. The shelves were also indeed stocked with books. Keyes reached for the nearest volume. It was thick, and grimy with grease from Oswald's cookery. He opened it to the title page and read:

D. IUNII IUVENALIS SATURAE XIII

Like many former Montrealers, Keyes had served time in a Jesuit school during his boyhood. Necessarily he had been given instruction in Latin. Much of it had melted away with the years of non-use, but enough remained to allow him to recognize what he held in his hand.

"Juvenal's Satires," he translated, as much for himself as for his companion.

"You don't say?" Joe muttered. "Lot of burger recipes in there, I'll bet."

Keyes did a quick inventory of the other books: Seneca, Virgil, Catullus, Propertius... Then he saw that the bookshelf was also a door: its frame fitted awkwardly into the wall at the back of the kitchen and looked as if it had never closed tightly, even when newly made.

"Home carpentry," he commented as he started to pull the clumsy structure open. Joe put a hand on his arm.

"Slow down," he said quietly. "Somebody around here has a homicidal streak, and there's a ready supply of knives and cleavers and what have you."

"That's all right— my belonophobia hasn't acted up in years," Keyes said.

Joe stared at him. "Skittish around lunch meat, are you, pal?"

"Well, Spam makes me nervous... sorry— belonophobia means being terrified of sharp instruments; Schopenhauer had something like it."

"Do tell?"

"Anyway, we have to find out if Oswald's behind this door, right?"

"We do, but let's go easy." Joe was rummaging around in drawers as he spoke. "There's got to be— yeah!" He triumphantly held up a ball of twine.

"Okay," Keyes said, catching Joe's drift, "but I think we're wasting our time— if he was in there we'd know about it by now."

"Do it to make an old guy happy."

Keyes nodded. He knew that Joe was right, in principle. Caution was eminently called for. He made a loop in the cord, slipped it over a hook that protruded from a shelf on which little French peas, raviolis, and three volumes of Momsen's *History of Rome* reposed. He pulled the loop tight, then paid out the twine as he backed out of the kitchen. Joe had preceded him, and was waiting behind the counter, holding the bottle from which they had been imbibing.

"Ready?" Keyes asked.

"One second," Joe said. He put the bottle to his lips and drained it, then flipped it, caught it by the neck, and held it over one shoulder like a club. "Ready."

Keyes pulled on the cord. A scraping sound came from the kitchen, followed by a thump and clatter that made both men jump. Then, silence. They looked at one another. Joe lowered his weapon as Keyes peeped around the corner. Books and tin cans covered the kitchen floor, and the little bookshelf door beyond stood open.

Joe peeped, too.

"Dark in there," he said.

"And empty."

"I suppose you're right," Joe agreed, but kept the bottle in his hand, clubwise.

Keyes crossed the kitchen, kicking aside cans as he went, but tried to avoid the books out of respect for antiquity or learning or something of the sort. He reached the opening that the bookshelf had disguised, and, standing to one side, looked in.

"Can't see a thing," he grumbled.

"Hold on," Joe said. "Be right back."

When Joe returned, he had a big, old-fashioned three-cell flashlight in his hand. Keyes took it, turned it on, and cast its strong beam about the interior of the shadowy space.

"No one home," he said.

They entered the room, no bigger than the kitchen. Smaller, in fact, because it was so crowded. Against the walls were book-packed shelves— the same rough shelves of which the door was constructed, shelves of scrap lumber and knocked-down packing cases. There were more books stacked on the floor. In the corner was a narrow cot, unmade. A bare lightbulb swayed gently from a cord in the ceiling above the cot. Keyes snapped it on.

There wasn't much else to see: a footlocker with some clothes in it, as unmade and messy as the bed, a chair with a sweatshirt tossed across it, a pair of fuzzy slippers, and a narrow window, shuttered and bolted from the inside.

Keyes stooped and scooped up a book; he wasn't surprised to find he held Titus Livius in his hand.

"I reckon Oswald must be out in the blizzard," Joe said.

"I reckon he must," Keyes agreed.

29.

"Where am I?"

Corinna sat up abruptly in her bed and stared wildly about. "The motel," she remembered, then giggled, "the Blue Bayou."

"Where's Claude?" she said, as if his pyjama top, which she was wearing, ought to be able to tell her.

"Oh right, he went back into the diner... I'll bet he's in there boozing." She tossed back the covers and swung her legs over the edge of the bed. "Well, I'm awake now... but I can't go out there like this," she muttered, glancing down at her bare thighs and the bareness below them.

Her rucksack lay beside her bed, open and with its contents spewed out. She rummaged in this heap until she found a pair of tights. She also found the boots she had worn the night before— it seemed such a long time ago— at The Rhinestone Cowperson.

"I didn't mean to bring these along," she said as she pulled an elaborately tooled boot onto her slender right foot. "Still, they are pretty."

Corinna stood up and strode to the mirror beside the door. There she practised her fast-draw several times.

"Too fast for you, Blackie!" she hissed at her reflection. "Your ass has had it! Pow! Pow!"

She pulled her overcoat off the hook where Keyes had hung it after she had dropped it casually to the cabin floor. "I'll just bet that coyote is drinking without me."

She pulled the coat close about her, opened the door, and marched out into the weather; the temperature had plummeted even further. Her boots were not tall enough to keep the snow out.

"Madre di Dios, hombre!" Corinna, the movie-goer, swore, pulling her collar tightly around her neck. "It's cold out here."

The diner was deserted when Corinna entered it. Belle was there, but dead and hidden by forever's maple leaf.

"Where is everybody?" Corinna murmured. "At least it's warm."

She took off her coat and tossed it into a booth.

"Hello," she called tentatively. "Anybody home?"

The wind outside gave a loud wail as she said this, obscuring her words, yowling, swallowing them up.

"I can't believe this weather. It's never this cold in Toronto. Bloody Wuthering Heights..." she paused, reflecting, then, editor that she was, found the *mot juste*. "Wuthering Flats, I mean."

Hoping to find a drink of something heartening, she stepped toward the counter.

"What the hell is that? It wasn't here when I left. The flag? This isn't a holiday, is it?"

She moved along the counter, put out her hand toward the flag-draped corpse, then drew back. A frisson toyed with the nape of her neck.

"It looks like... but that's silly. It can't be."

Her native boldness returned and she put out the hand again to lift a corner of the red and white bunting. Belle's dead face, eyes not quite closed despite the ministrations of Moanin' Joe McKendricks, looked up at her.

Corinna shrieked.

Keyes and McKendricks scrambled out of Oswald's den, stumbling over one another, back into the diner.

"Are you all right?" Keyes shouted, less sympathetically than he might have intended. "Did anyone...?"

"What is that?" Corinna demanded, pointing an accusatory forefinger at Belle. "Never mind. I know what it is. How did it happen?"

Joe stepped close to her. "You're okay, though? Didn't see anybody?"

Corinna drew away from the cowboy, stared witheringly at him, then spoke again to Keyes.

"What is going on? Is that woman dead... or...?" Her bravado failed her for a moment. "She looks... dead."

Keyes nodded. "She is."

"Shot," Joe added. "Square in the heart, by the look of it."

Again Corinna ignored the cowboy.

"Jean-Claude, what have you gotten us into?"

"Me?"

"I didn't mean that," Corinna muttered. "This is horrible... that poor woman. But who...?"

She looked uncomfortably about the bleak diner.

"Who...?" she echoed.

"No idea," Keyes said. "We got here after it happened. The back door was open and I went out to see..."

"That was foolish of you. He might have been armed."

Joe nodded. "That's what I figured. J.C. knows no fear, or maybe he just doesn't have any horse sense."

Corinna looked levelly at Joe. "On the contrary, my friend has very good sense... usually." Then she turned to Keyes: "What were you thinking, Claude? This man could have shot you, too."

Keyes made a strange face. "We don't know that the killer is a man..."

"Likely, though," Joe put in.

"What makes you say that?" Corinna snapped. "You didn't see him, did you?"

"Nope."

"Well, then."

Keyes adjusted the drapery to cover Belle's face again.

"I didn't see anybody. It could have been... I think we should talk to the others. Warn them that there's somebody with a gun out there."

"The others?" Corinna said. "You mean the people here in the motel? Oh, my God, it could be one of them."

"Not likely," Joe said. "They were all here by accident... because of the storm."

"Still..."

"She's right, Joe," Keyes said. "Anyway, we better get them back in here."

"Safety in numbers," Corinna agreed. "Did you call the cops?"

"Tried," Keyes said. "Phones still aren't working..."

"I'll go round everybody up," Joe said, getting into his coat. "We're lucky we still got hydro," he commented. Hardly were the words out of his mouth when the lights flickered, died, then came back on again. Joe shook his head ruefully, jammed his black hat far down over his eyes, and made for the door to the stormy world outside.

Corinna looked after him.

"I don't trust that man, Claude," she said.

"I sort of noticed that, but you don't trust most men."

"With good reason! But I trust *you*."

"You know I don't carry a gun. Look, you trust me, and I trust Joe. Does that change your opinion at all?"

"No," Corinna said firmly. She then inexplicably produced

her paperback novel from somewhere and hid her face behind it, but Keyes could see that particular sort of unfocussed look in her eyes which indicated that she was involved in some other, more personal, narrative. At last she put the book away again and looked at Keyes. "My father was a man like that—"

"A country singer?" asked Keyes, amazed.

"No," Corinna denied emphatically. "A musician. He played the French horn, but he could never hold down a steady position with any of the symphonies— he said he was too 'avant-garde' for them, too experimental, that he preferred to freelance... truth is, he was too fond of expensive clothes and trampy cello players..."

"Was he a good horn player?" Keyes asked, uncertain what else might be appropriate under the circumstances.

"The best," Corinna admitted. "At least that's what my mother always says. I never heard him play, not even when he practised— his rehearsal room was soundproofed, and it was off-limits to children, especially his own."

"Were you and your mother... I mean, did he abandon you?"

Corinna shook her head. "Not in the traditional sense. There was always a little money, and he and Mom never even separated. When he wasn't on the road he lived in the same house with us, but he was always either rehearsing his music, or talking about it..."

"Well, musicians and people who love music tend to be passionate," Keyes said. It sounded lame, even to him, but he was thinking of his own mother's devotion to opera. He had to admit, though, that this had never interfered with her devotion to her son.

"Hmph," Corinna snorted. "My father and his *passions*... I met one of them once, by accident— big-boobed, bottled blonde, too much perfume, and even *I* could play a better cello!"

"You play the cello?" Although Keyes knew his editor and friend to be multi-talented, this was the first he had heard about this particular skill.

"Not any more— I gave it up when I was twelve, which was when I figured out all this stuff about my father; I guess I made some kind of subconscious connection between that particular instrument and cheap sluts," Corinna said, with a bitterness Keyes had rarely heard from her. He decided it was time to divert the conversation in another direction.

"What did your mother do?" he asked.

"She was a flautist," Corinna said, then laughed sadly. "Maybe that was her mistake..."

30.

McKendricks struggled against the wind that roared across the parking lot onto which the guest units faced. Even before he knocked on the first door, another down the line popped open. Two men staggered out of number six: Fred, blue with cold, and George, red with rage. They didn't bother to acknowledge the presence of the tall figure of Moanin' Joe, but bolted past him, ragged blankets flapping like cloaks behind them.

Joe watched them pass. When he was sure they were inside the diner, he rapped on the first door he came to. Louise De Wetering opened it, her arm cocked and ready to deliver a punch with all of her considerable strength behind it.

"Whoa, lady!" Joe yelled, backing quickly away.

"Sorry," Louise said. "I thought you were somebody else."

"I'm sure as hell pleased I'm somebody other'n who you thought I was!"

Shouting to be heard above the wind, Joe explained the situation in the diner. "I think you better come in," he concluded, "and bring the kid with you."

"She's had a rough day."

"Might get rougher if she stays out here by herself."

"I guess you're right."

"I am... once in while."

He waited at the door, his back hunched against the weather until Louise had roused, dressed, and hurried Jennet into the relative security of the main building.

In unit four he found only Gordy Doig.

"Where's your partner?" Joe demanded, glancing suspiciously around the small room.

Gordy looked uneasy, guilty. "He... went outside."

"Outside? In this mess? What for?"

"I dunno..."

The cowboy was sure that Gordy did know, but he was too cold to challenge the roadworker right at that particular moment. He quickly explained about Belle instead.

"Shot?" Gordy gasped. He had liked the woman— she'd reminded him a little of his friend Midge in the office, except a few years older.

"You better get in there."

As was generally the case with Gordy Doig, he did what he was told.

Hawkwind was sitting where Joe had left him in unit three, except that his motorcycle was now resting on its kickstand in the middle of the rug in a puddle of melted snow. The air in the room was even heavier with pleasantly sweet-smelling smoke. The biker was gently mumbling something– he had reached the mantra stage. He glanced up as Joe entered, then cast a gentle look at his Yamaha as he spoke to McKendricks.

"She was cold," he said. "Na myoho renge kyo..."

Joe couldn't help grinning. "You sure are a true democrat where religion's concerned, son!" He didn't try to explain what had happened. He just got Hawkwind up, pointed to the diner and gave him a gentle push in its direction. Hawkwind followed the rhythm of Joe's actions as if it was all part of a great cosmic pattern which only he understood. The mantra never ceased.

There was no answer at first when Joe knocked on unit five's door. Finally, there was a scuffling sound inside, and then a sleepy, girlish voice, asking what on earth was the matter. Joe told her what was the matter through the door, yelling at the top of his voice. Again he waited in the snow, this time until Mrs. Cook and Mrs. Baker appeared, huddled together under a single blanket. Their chubby knees appeared every now and then from between the folds of the bedspread, like tiny bald heads. The two women were strangely distracted.

"Did you say 'dead?'" Darlene asked dreamily, as the three of them headed back towards the diner.

"Did he say 'dead,' dear?" Earlene echoed with equal lightness.

"Dead!" Joe bellowed above the gale.

31.

The travellers made a forlorn and motley band once they were assembled in the diner. No one had known what to wear for this grim gathering. Getting from the units to the diner demanded heavy coats, mufflers, caps, and boots, but the urgency of a murder had resulted in a certain disarray beneath the winter wear. Darlene and Earlene were hardly dressed at all, only bundled about with blankets. Jennet had put her hair up in a tousled knot on top her head that made her look older than her years. Louise had stripped to T-shirt and tights in the cabin, and came to the diner that way except for the addition of a leather jacket tossed across her monumental shoulders. George and Fred looked even more foolish than usual, with their cruise clothes flashing loudly from beneath shredded bits of bedding. Gordy Doig, accustomed to working outdoors, had come without a coat. Only Hawkwind was constant: his leather biker's uniform was intact, fashion-proof, and situation-proof.

Moanin' Joe drew aside from the others, and leaned against a post close to the door, perhaps to be on guard in case someone should try to bolt from the room or to storm in from the outside.

Everyone else stood restlessly in the middle of the floor. Some had the grace to glance only once at the pathetic little heap on the counter, while others stared like children in a candy store.

Keyes noticed that only Jennet did not look at all in the direction of the corpse, and wondered whether to attribute this lack of curiosity to a youthful show of nonchalance, or to terror.

"Couldn't find Doig's sidekick," Joe McKendricks reported.

Keyes looked at Gordy Doig.

"Where's your friend?" Keyes asked.

"Peavine's not my friend, exactly," Gordy said hastily. "We just work together."

"But where *is* he?"

"Outside somewhere— he went for a walk."

"In this weather?"

"That's what he said."

"I think I'm going to be sick," Corinna muttered suddenly.

Keyes, ever the gentleman, held out a useless hand. "Better lie down," he said helplessly.

Louise stepped forward and took Corinna's arm.

"Come on, honey," she said. "You can curl up in one of the booths."

Corinna wilted against the big woman.

"Thanks, Miss... Miss..." She broke off since she didn't know her benefactor's name.

"Call me Louise."

"I'm not used to this sort of thing," Corinna said in a voice much smaller than the one she usually employed. "That poor woman..."

"Not used to it, eh?" Despite the ironic tone of her voice, Louise behaved well. She obviously did not find Corinna much to her taste, but she conducted the sick editor to a corner and made her sit down.

"We have murders down here all the time," she said, as she covered Corinna with the coat Keyes passed to her. "All the time. Perth County is renowned for its murders, at least on the stage."

Corinna moaned and put her head down.

Keyes looked at Joe, as if to say: "Now what?"

Joe shrugged and shook his head.

Keyes cleared his throat nervously. He knew this feeling. It was called stage fright. He had experienced it often enough during his youthful acting career. He didn't like the feeling and had left the stage to get away from it.

"Now what?" George Cook demanded.

Keyes took the cue. He stepped forward a pace or so, found a warm spot beneath the lights, and played his part.

"You've heard what happened," he began tentatively, wishing he had a text to work from. "The proprietress has been shot. We've no idea why, or by whom..."

He glanced at Joe to include him in the "we," to keep his speech from being too imperial. Not very helpfully, Joe looked at the floor.

"We thought it would be better," Keyes continued doggedly, "if we were all together until this gets sorted out."

"There's somebody around with a gun, probably something like a .22 calibre pistol," Joe put in. "Somebody who might try using it again."

"But not," Keyes hurried to add, "if we're watching out for one another."

"I need a drink," Fred said.

This admission was followed by a chorus of "right on"s and "me, too"s.

"I'll get a bottle," Joe said, going to the counter where Belle lay. "I don't guess she'll grudge us a little of her booze."

"Specially not on such a cold night," Louise put in.

"Do you think it might be... somebody here?" Darlene asked.

Keyes shook his head. "I don't know what to think."

"But it could be," Darlene pursued. "One of us."

"I suppose so. Did any of you see anything?"

"What do you mean by 'anything?'" Earlene murmured, as if she, for one, had seen rather a lot in the last hour.

"Well, anything suspicious."

The travellers shuffled uneasily, looking around the room, looking unbelievingly at each other.

Joe returned with the promised bottle and a stack of glasses which he deftly deposited on a table.

"Settle down, people," he said heartily. "No point in standing up all night."

"I don't drink," Jennet said.

"I hope not," Joe said, "a kid like you. I'll find a cola or something."

"Juice, please."

"Juice, then." He returned to the counter, rummaged beneath it, and came up with a bottle.

"Something called Orangina here."

Jennet nodded. Still she did not look at the flag-draped form on the counter.

One by one, or in pairs, as was the case with Earlene and Darlene, the travellers did what Joe had called "settling down." Most sat at tables; Hawkwind withdrew to a booth. A hush fell over the room as Keyes set the glasses out, a hush that was gently broken by the consoling sound of rye whiskey being poured.

Corinna's head popped up.

"I know that sound," she said.

"Feeling better, sweetie?" Louise asked.

"Thanks, I am. Would you mind calling me by my name?"

"I could try... if I knew what it was."

"Oh, of course... Corinna Brand."

"Say again?"

Corinna said again.

"Funny name. You from Nova Scotia or something?"

Corinna smiled weakly and went to scoop up a glass. The

others followed her example, some more eagerly than others.

Hawkwind remained in his corner.

"Not drinking, kid?" Joe called over to him.

The biker frowned. "Not that shit, man. Bad juju."

Joe shrugged. It was his most characteristic gesture. "Nobody's got any manners nowadays," he murmured.

"Well, then," Corinna said, obviously much refreshed by her little rest and the whiskey, "what next?"

"I'm not sure," Keyes replied. He glanced at a window. "It's still snowing. We can't go anywhere."

"You called the police, didn't you?" George said.

"I tried. The lines are still down," Keyes told him.

"Or maybe the killer sabotaged them before we got here."

Joe mused on sabotage. "I don't think so. I think it's the weather."

George took offense. "You know something the rest of us don't?"

"It's the .22," Joe said. "Not, in my experience, the weapon of a man who knows much about sabotaging telephone lines in the middle of a blizzard."

"What makes you so sure it's a man?" Corinna asked. "A .22 is small, isn't it? A woman's gun..."

"*I* own a .38," Louise said, "an old Police Special— and *I'm* a woman."

Gordy Doig, who had been silent through all of this, got shakily to his feet.

"There's a radio in the truck," he announced.

All heads turned toward him; all eyes fixed on him.

"You took your time telling us," George Cook said.

"Where's the truck?" Keyes said.

"Right outside," Doig answered. "It doesn't work, though."

"The truck?" George muttered.

"No, the radio."

"Well, then," said Keyes, "it looks like we're on our own."

32.

"So, what do we do all night?" George Cook said in his surly way. "Sit around and wait for someone to confess or take a potshot at one of *us*?"

Keyes had been thinking about this very thing, and had been trying to figure a way to bring up his solution naturally. George had thoughtfully given him a cue. Keyes found himself slipping into the more formal phrasing and careful diction of an actor as he laid out his admittedly jury-rigged plan.

"I have a suggestion that will pass the time, and might also be of some use to the police, when we're able to contact them," Keyes said, trying his best not to sound as if he had taken complete control of the proceedings, although he *had* once wanted to direct. "The authorities will most certainly want statements from all of us, so I thought that it might be efficient if we took care of those now, while everything is fresh in our minds. I have this tape recorder..." He pulled the device from his jacket pocket and held it up for all to see. "... and it struck me that it might be helpful if we each tell who we are, and where we were before Joe and I found Belle, and anything else that might be pertinent..."

He did not add that the whole exercise might also make those present feel much more at ease if it could be established that no one in the room was guilty of the crime. Keyes glanced at the several pairs of eyes focused on him, to see how his recommendation was being received. Joe, Corinna, and Louise were nodding in agreement; Gordy Doig seemed to not quite comprehend what was being proposed. Hawkwind had his eyes shut and was humming to himself; Darlene and Earlene were staring at one another. Fred Baker was nodding his head, but at something George had whispered to him, rather than in concurrence with Keyes' suggestion. Jennet's expression was neutral, unreadable.

George spoke first. "I don't want anything to do with this amateur detective stuff. I'll talk to the cops when the time comes. I know where Fred was and he knows where I was. End of story." He crossed his arms firmly across his chest in a time-honoured pose of he-man defiance. Fred echoed his friend's move.

"Let's do it," Joe said. "I'll go first, if you want."

Keyes flashed a grateful look at his stage manager, set the compact cassette machine on a nearby table, then flicked the RECORD switch. Joe sat down across from the machine, and, as people will do, spoke a bit more loudly than normal, staring at the gadget as if it were a person with eyes to look into.

"Joseph Milton McKendricks, musician and traveller. I'm closer to fifty years old than forty, originally from Sackville, New Brunswick, but I consider myself a native of the whole nation of Canada... I was on a bus bound for Stratford to play three nights at a place called the Wabash-Canon Bar & Grill, got storm-stayed here at the Blue Bayou. At the time we think this poor woman, Belle, was shot, I was in the room she'd kindly assigned to me, with a young fella goes by the handle of Hawkwind... guess you'll hear from him later... he was with me, as I'm sure he'll tell you himself. Was me first found the body, me and a Mr. Claude Keyes, chap who owns this recording widget..." Joe trailed off, and looked at Keyes. "Can't think of anything else." He got up and returned to his watcher post in a corner.

Keyes cast a questioning eye at the others. Darlene and Earlene glared at their husbands, then stood up together, and, hand in hand, approached the table, and leaned over the recorder.

"Hello?" Darlene said to the silver box. "I was with my friend, Earlene."

"That's right," Earlene said, leaning so close to the machine that she appeared to be giving it a kiss. "We were with each other. I'll swear to that in court."

Both women were blushing, and Keyes was beginning to have slight and charming suspicions based on their altered attitude toward one another and current mode of semi-dress. He suspected that Rubens and Sappho would approve of the transformed Darlene Cook and Earlene Baker. They returned to their seats. Their husbands glared at *them*.

Corinna took the recording stand next, describing herself and her movements with clear precision, although her voice quavered.

Gordy Doig's voice shook as well during his rambling testimony, especially when he told of Peavine's inexplicable desire to go for a stroll, as if he felt disloyal at being unable to provide an alibi for his partner.

Louise De Wetering's narration was as straightforward and attentive to detail as had been Corinna's, although without quite the same richness of vocabulary.

"I've driven this same route for a few years," she said, "and got to know Belle Feist— the murdered woman— a little bit. I liked her. She was tough, and funny, and a real straight-shooter... She'd had problems with men— who hasn't?— some her fault, some not; and it's kind of strange, but during all that time, I never met her husband, Oswald. He never came out of the kitchen, not while I was in the place, and I never heard him actually *say* anything— he'd talk to Belle with this kind of goofy drumming on pots and pans and stuff. Belle told me he used to be a teacher, but he'd had some kind of car accident, suffered brain damage... she wouldn't give details, just said it made things difficult. But she swore that she didn't have any regrets, except that every now and then she wished she'd had another baby. I don't know what she meant by 'another,' and she wouldn't say anything about that, either; just shook her head, and said, 'water under the bridge, Louise, and I don't want to drown in it.'"

Louise stopped talking, but did not move: she was trying to decide whether this was the time to mention the peeping incident with Peavine Choate, and at last, sticking to her own personal code of ethics, concluded that there was no real need— she had settled with the creep there and then, and until further informa- tion warranted disclosure, she would leave it at that; copping a cheap peek at a naked woman did not make a man a killer in Louise's book, although it might make *him* dead if she caught him again. If Jennet wanted to bring it up, that was her business.

"That's it, I guess," Louise concluded, and made way for her young friend.

Jennet said, "I was with Louise," and nothing else.

Keyes now sat before the recorder and told his story. He noticed Corinna making exasperated faces at him during his monologue, and grinned to himself: she was always attempting to cure what she called his gratuitous affair with adjectives and adverbs. "To pad is human, to delete divine," she had told him on many occasions, especially while applying her gifted red pen to his deathless prose.

Finally, Keyes motioned to Hawkwind, who came from his cross-legged position to his feet like a cobra uncoiling, and did a hop, skip, and jump to the table, where he bent over the table as closely as Earlene had. He made some sort of adjustment to the recorder, then lowered his voice and whispered into the microphone grille for a minute or so. No one, not even Keyes, who was only a few feet away, heard a word he said. Then he straightened, looked at Keyes, said "Bathroom," and strode off in the direction of the facilities.

"I guess that does it," Keyes said as he hit the OFF toggle. "Thanks for cooperating."

With the cessation of the recording, the Blue Bayou became very quiet, as if an entire squadron of angels was passing through the clouds and snow above.

33.

"Then that means," Corinna said slowly, "it can't be one of us?"

"Apparently," Keyes agreed. "If we've all got alibis."

Gordy Doig looked uncomfortable.

"Except me and Peavine," he murmured. "But I just can't believe... He's a bit scary, and he's done time, but only for being drunk and disorderly."

"Was he drunk tonight?" Joe asked.

"Not *that* drunk," Doig insisted, shaking his head emphatically. "Not as drunk as I've seen him sometimes."

"Drunk or not," Louise said, "the sonuvabitch was sure as

hell disorderly... but he does have an alibi— me; I caught him peeping in our window while the kid and me weren't decent. The sick fuck was right there, grinning in at us—"

"She socked him one, right through the glass!" Jennet interrupted.

"I guess I owe somebody for a window—" Louise broke off abruptly, frowning heavily.

"What is it?" Keyes asked. "What's the matter?"

"I just remembered something that clinches it."

"Remembered what?"

"It was just before that that I heard it."

"Heard it? Heard the gunshot, you mean?"

Louise nodded. "Our room is closest to the diner. You remember, Jen? We both heard this sound and looked toward the window. That's when we saw peeping Peavine."

Jennet's eyes were very big.

"I did," she said in a voice husky and uncertain as the voice of an adolescent boy. "I did hear it."

"So Peavine has an alibi, too," Keyes concluded.

"Why?" Fred said. "He was out there. He's the only one..."

"He was at Louise's window when the shot was fired."

"Not even Annie Oakley could make a shot like that," Corinna said, proud of her western lore.

"Anyway, he isn't the only one," Keyes went on. "You're forgetting Oswald."

"Oswald... Who's Oswald?" Fred said.

"The cook— Belle's husband."

"I didn't see a cook..."

"No, but you heard him. We all heard him."

There was a chorus of affirmative sounds: words, gasps, grunts, but all affirmative.

"Oswald... of course," Corinna said.

Keyes shook his head thoughtfully.

"Not necessarily Oswald *of course*, I'm afraid," he said. "Oswald *maybe*..."

"But..."

George Cook was about to put his unpleasant seven cents worth into the conversation, but before he could, the door burst open, the gale roared into the diner, the gale and the snow, and in the midst of it stood a creature new and strange to the reluctant guests at the Blue Bayou. He, or it, was dragging something behind him.

34.

Froste himself, Keyes thought; his already fertile imagination, palpated to a frenzy by adrenaline and tension, had conjured up the leader of the evil ice giants who had plagued Wotan and crew throughout Norse eternity. The newcomer, although grotesquely decorated with ice and snow in elaborate shapes and patterns, was far from gigantic. The man was a few inches shorter than average, but very broad and blockish.

After a brief tableau of astonishment, it was Gordy who reacted as he recognized what, or rather whom, the iceman was dragging.

"Peavine!" he shouted, and took a half-step forward, then retraced the step, loyalty having been overcome by prudence.

Keyes and Joe moved toward the intruder a second later, but, unlike Gordy, they did not stop— both Keyes and Joe had spotted the small and most un-Viking-like weapon in the stranger's ham-sized left hand. Keyes grabbed and squeezed the thick wrist which held the .22, while Joe seized the right hand, which was gripping Peavine's collar. The man finally let go of his burdens; Peavine's head and the handgun hit the floor with a *thump* and a *clunk*, respectively. Then, the snow-covered bogeyman whom Keyes and Joe held between them spoke, and when Keyes heard the language, his fragile frost giant metaphor collapsed completely.

"Pedicabo ego uous et irrumabo Aureli pathice et cinaede Furi!"[6]

The voice was a high and pure tenor, rather than the deep basso which Keyes would have expected from such a cavernous chest, and the words were enunciated clearly and (as nearly as anyone there could tell) correctly. Keyes strongly suspected that this apparition was the inhabitant of the book-lined back room.

"I'm not sure," Keyes said to Joe, "but I think we've just been insulted, and rudely at that."

Their prisoner made a seemingly effortless shrugging movement and Keyes and Joe, both tall men, and strong enough under most circumstances, were flung toward the nearby wall. There were assorted screams and shouts from the onlookers. Leaving Peavine on the floor, the former captive turned away from all of them and walked stiffly over to the counter.

Slowly, he slid the flag from Belle's face with a gentleness surprising to his audience, who were still in the process of judging him by his appearance. The melting of the frost from his features was not an improvement: his face was heavily jowled and shadowed with beard stubble, while receding and wispy black hair over

---

6. "Aurelius, you cunt, fuck you! Furius, you faggot, suck my dick!"

heavy eyebrows gave him the demeanour of the oft-reported but never verified Missing Link. His walk, however, was straight-backed and proud, even regal, now that he was no longer dragging Peavine.

He stared down at Belle, and Keyes could see that the ice water dripping down the wide face was mixed with tears. The big hands reached across Belle's body, then drew back, holding two long-handled wooden spoons, which were soon beating against the counter edge with the stately *thump-bump-bump-a-thump* of a funeral march.

Keyes looked at Joe. "Oswald," he said. Joe's hat bobbed in agreement.

Oswald Feist looked up at the sound of his name, and he, too, nodded. Keyes moved toward him, warily; there was a tender spot on Keyes' left shoulder where it had been abruptly introduced to the wall, and he had no wish to try for bilateral symmetry in bruises.

"Oswald...?" Keyes began, searching for the least confrontational method of phrasing a question which could be nothing but tactless, under the circumstances. "Did you... kill your wife?" That was subtle, Keyes! he berated himself instantly.

Oswald's head snapped back and forth in the negative so vigorously that Keyes thought the man might dislocate his neck. Oswald's right arm trembled violently as he pointed a wooden spoon toward the supine Peavine. Oswald's whole body became agitated, especially his huge, homely face. His lips pursed and flapped, labouring to form words, while his liquid brown gaze darted from Keyes to corpse to kitchen, as if seeking the aid of his books. He drummed his spoons against his own thighs with epileptic violence. At last, a flurry of phrases escaped his twitching mouth:

"Adeste, hendecasyllabi, quot estis... omnes undique, quotquot estis omnes!"[7]

Keyes had never seen eyes quite so filled with fright as Oswald's were just before he collapsed to the floor in a heap beside Belle's formica catafalque, a few feet away from Peavine.

Oh, Christ, Keyes thought irrelevantly, we might as well be doing *Hamlet*— there are people falling all over the stage!

Keyes and Joe hurried to squat beside the now unconscious Oswald. The rest looked on with varying degrees of interest ranging from concerned to morbid. Only Jennet was paying no heed to Oswald at all, but instead was staring fixedly across the room at Belle's exposed face. Jennet seemed to come to some kind of decision, perhaps concluding that today was as good a day as any to look Thanatos in the face, although she would not have called Death by so grand a name. It requires more than the sixteen years she had so far served in her life sentence to become aware of the chameleon nature of the Reaper, to know that he (or she) has many names, and is not always grim or cold, or even readily identified.

The girl, as had Oswald before her, approached the counter and stared down into Belle's face. Jennet's head cocked slightly to one side, as if she were observing a formaldehyde-soaked frog in biology class. Keyes glanced up at her, content to let Joe minister to the fallen Oswald. Keyes then saw Jennet's expression of detached calm give way to something more immediate, and so intimate that Keyes was embarrassed to be observing it. He felt like a psychic voyeur peeping at spiritual nudity through a

---

7. "Help, I need eleven syllables! Any kinds of syllables, all kinds of syllables!"

momentary keyhole in the walls which separate human beings. When Jennet spoke, it was to Belle, in a voice rich with wonder and surprise:

"You look just like her," Jennet said. "The sleeping woman who protects me... in my dreams..."

Then she turned away from the corpse, and her eyes looked into Keyes' with a gaze of deep need which asked, "What does this mean?"

Keyes had no ready answer to her silent plea; in any event, a sudden groan of returning consciousness from Oswald caused the spotlight of his attention to shift again.

Keyes put an arm under Oswald's burly shoulders to assist him in sitting up.

"Keep a weather eye on him," Joe cautioned.

"He doesn't look dangerous," Keyes said. "Doesn't even particularly look like a murderer..."

"Who does?" Joe snorted. "I knew this guy once—"

"Not now, Joe!" Keyes snapped. "He's trying to say something."

"... didn't... kill... anybody..." Oswald said with excruciating slowness. The words came like a tape recording speeding up, or like the vocal equivalent of the first halting steps of someone who has been confined to a wheelchair for a very long time and is beginning to walk again; there was also a distortion in his pronunciation which held a trace of the Latin Oswald had declaimed just before his collapse.

"Can you tell us what happened?" Keyes prompted gently, then went on to supply cues. "If you didn't kill her, why did you have the gun?"

Joe, meanwhile, rummaged about until he found plastic sandwich bags and a pair of stainless-steel tongs. He slipped the weapon into a bag with the same economy of motion with which he rolled cigarettes or played the guitar.

"... found... it," Oswald mumbled. "After I found... Belle... dead... gun was beside her... picked it up to... get *him*..." He pointed at Peavine. "He was... outside, blood on his face... *He* did it!"

Keyes shook his head. "He has an alibi, Oswald. He's no candidate for sainthood, but he didn't kill Belle..."

"Was *somebody*," Oswald continued. "I heard... the door... there were footprints... *somebody* dropped the... gun on the floor..."

Keyes stood suddenly, and snapped his fingers. "The station wagon!"

"What?"

"What station wagon?"

"What's he talking about?"

Keyes hurried to the window. It was still there, nearly buried beneath the snow, but still there nonetheless, the big vehicle which he had noticed earlier while on the way to his room.

"Does anybody know whose car that is?"

There was a jumble of confusion and whispering as heads craned to see the visible portion of the vehicle, partially obscured by Louise's bus as well as by snow. Only Jennet had not joined them; she remained unmoving at her post beside Belle.

No one identified the car, and, for completeness' sake if nothing else, Keyes went to Jennet and gently insisted that she have a look. Keyes had expected the same negative response as from the others, and took a step back in surprise at the suddenness and intensity of her response.

"No!" Jennet cried out. "He can't be here! I'll never get away from him!"

"*Now* what's going on?"

"What *is* that girl talking about?"

"Who?"

Louise took Jennet's shoulders firmly. "Calm down. It's whatshisname, isn't it? Your stepfather?"

"Yes."

Louise, keeping one arm around Jennet, quickly recapped what Jennet had told her about the girl's flight from the sexual advances of Burgess Cassell. All of the women were immediately indignant and upset, and flowed around Jennet in a warm knot of solicitude and support. The men looked vaguely embarrassed. Keyes became very angry indeed.

"Look," he said at last, "we can't go anywhere, but if this guy's still around the building, he can't hurt us as long as we stay together— I don't think. It was probably Cassell that Oswald went after, and if he's out in that storm..." There was no need for Keyes to go on; no one would get very far on foot in the blizzard; survival itself was doubtful without arctic expertise and properly protective clothing. "For now, I suggest we do what we can for Oswald... and Peavine; they're here, and they're alive."

There was general agreement with Keyes' practicality, and soon they had Oswald seated in a booth with a cup of coffee in front of him. Peavine had come around, and sat woozily in a corner, as far away from Oswald (and from Louise) as possible.

Finally, when Oswald had recovered somewhat, Joe approached him.

"That your library back there?" he asked, jerking a thumb toward the kitchen. Oswald nodded. "What's with the Latin, friend? And the—" Joe slapped his palms against the table, *thump-ditty-rat-at-at.* Keyes tried to get Joe's attention, to discourage him from grilling the poor man, who had, after all, just lost his wife, but Oswald was eager to talk, perhaps to divert his mind from that very fact. There is never any way to predict how a particular individual will react to tragedy, especially an individual as enigmatic as Oswald Feist.

35.

"I met Lesb— *Belle*— Braddock... in London," Oswald said, "at the University of Western... Ontario... eleven...? years ago. I was a teaching assistant, in charge of a night course for part-time students... Introductory Latin. I was a Catullus scholar... Belle was one of my students, trying to 'improve herself,' as they say. We fell in love..."

Oswald's speech was growing more confident, the diction more regular, the halting to grasp for words less frequent. It was like turning on the hot-water tap, with the temperature of the water continuing to increase until it reached its optimum. His voice now sounded quite pleasant to Keyes, who recognized a trace of the lecturer in its rhythms.

"We got married. We were happy; I was, certainly, and Belle seemed content... except when she thought about the child she'd had when she was a teenager... she had to give the baby up because she was simply not ready, and she felt it would have a better chance somewhere else... She wasn't obsessed, but sometimes the memory would ambush her. It made her very sad. And it was even harder on her when we found out that I was sterile... a blessing, as it turned out. But she never complained. Never complained... and then... I had... the accident." Keyes heard the empty and bottomless void of the abyss open up in the long sigh and pause which punctuated Oswald's sentence.

"The Classics Department was having a small party to celebrate the opening of an exhibit devoted to the reign of Claudius... I was doing double duty, master of ceremonies and drumming with my weekend rock band, The Changelings— I'd booked us as the evening's entertainment... the older faculty members were not amused, but the rest of us were having a wonderful time, especially Belle... my colleagues and students thought the world of her. Anyway, I was pounding away on the drum solo to *In-A-Gadda-Da-Vida*... when I felt a terrible, terrible pain against my head, and the lights went out— my lights. There was a large statuette of Messalina mounted behind me, and the vibrations from the music had shaken it loose... it hit me square on the head... I never did have much use for Messalina."

From behind them, Keyes heard George Cook mutter loudly, "Who the hell's Messy Leena?" Corinna glared the man into silence. Oswald continued.

"I was in a coma for three weeks. Apparently I was fortunate to live... But my brain— my memory— had been damaged in a way that no one quite understood: my linguistic abilities were completely scrambled— when I could find the mental strength to speak at all, it was only in quotations from Catullus' poetry, that I'd been immersed in at the time— I was working on a new translation, for my Master's..."

"But you were aware of what was going on around you? Of your situation? Your condition?" Keyes asked, fascinated and horrified at the same time. Oswald shook his head.

"No. I'm remembering it clearly *now*... but as if it happened to someone else, with me watching, only from the inside— I can't explain it any better than that. I was frustrated most of the time, attempting to find quotations that matched what I was trying to communicate; when that failed, I lapsed into a sort of personal, percussive Morse code, and I spoke to no one but Belle. She could understand the Latin and the drumming, most of the time. I was angry... but Belle was amazing. She found a lawyer who was able to prove that the workman who had installed the statuette in its niche had been negligent— drunk, I think— and we received a settlement. Enough to move to Stratford and buy this place, do some renovating. It all more or less worked out... until... now."

Oswald stopped abruptly, and his head swivelled toward Belle once more. There were fresh tears in the huge brown eyes. Keyes' own dilemma with his house and publishing contract suddenly seemed very simple, very small.

Oswald's larger-and-weirder-than-life tale might have been one of Moanin' Joe McKendricks' surreal fables, and it had both mesmerized and upset Keyes to the point where he automatically poked around in his pocket for the comfort of the cigarettes he no longer carried. Instead, his hand came up with the bundle of envelopes he had discovered among the detritus after Belle's demise. He held the packet out to Oswald, explaining how it had come into his possession.

"Her letters to her daughter—" Oswald began to explain, but Jennet interrupted him, in a barely audible voice.

"Letters?" the girl said. "I have a letter... the only contact I ever had with my real mother..." From her own pocket she produced a sheet of paper which she set on the table beside the others. It became slowly obvious to Keyes, and to anyone else with eyes to see and wit to comprehend, what had been going through the young girl's mind as she had studied Belle's body so intently. Had Jennet found her lost mother? Keyes found himself wishing that this were so, but in the court of Fate, the letters were evidence to the contrary: there was no match that Keyes could see, either in the stationery or the handwriting, but it was Oswald who pointed out, in a gentle teacher's voice, the main discrepancy.

"Belle was... rough-spoken, but she was an impeccable speller," he said, "and in this, well..." His voice trailed off as he waved Jennet's letter; Oswald obviously had no wish to insult Jennet's vision of her mother. Jennet slowly took back the tattered sheet of paper, and returned it carefully to her pocket. Her expression was melancholy. "Oh, baby..." whispered Corinna and Louise together.

Keyes started to speak as well, but did not: what could he possibly say that would provide any comfort to a young girl who, while fleeing, if not for her life, at least for her honour and self-worth, had grabbed at a small brass ring of hope, only to find that it was an illusion? Nothing, Keyes decided. Words, in any language, at this moment, were worthless. It was a feeling that seemed to be shared all around.

Finally, Joe broke the silence.

"Anybody know what happened to Hawkwind?" he asked.

36.

Hawkwind soared, on every plane of his being, both physical and metaphysical. As the motorcycle bucked and bounced along the ice-slick highway, kept upright only by Hawkwind's skill and his faith, so his thoughts leapt in synchronization with the machine.

He could not really say why he had left the motel abruptly

and secretively through the bathroom window, except that he had been summoned. Voices often spoke to Hawkwind, from the sky, from inside cookie packages, and often from the engine block of his Yamaha. They were friendly voices, and he tended to take their advice or orders seriously, except when on occasion they told him to do something exceptionally stupid or dangerous— these commands Hawkwind ignored as happily as he obeyed their more enjoyable marching orders.

The voice in the Blue Bayou had sung to him in a sweet soprano from the cassette recorder into which he was speaking at the request of one of the men there who had befriended him. "Come north," it had said. "Come north, come north..."

And so he was going north. His family lived in Sudbury. It had been a long time since he had seen them.

Then, about a mile from the Blue Bayou, a shape coalesced out of the snowfall, directly in front of the hurtling bike. Hawkwind's wrists and body shifted instinctively to avoid the obstacle. The Yamaha swerved and went into a skid, but Hawkwind did not lose control, and he missed hitting the apparition by inches. When he was back on course, he glanced over his shoulder. There was nothing to see but pure white twisting curtains of snow.

"Mutant rabbit?" Hawkwind muttered, and continued on his way.

37.

Cassell ran with all his might. It seemed to him that he had been running for a very long time. He had. The storm blew as fiercely as ever, raking him with its winds, blasting him with ice and snow. He had no idea where his car was, or what he meant to accomplish by running. He knew only that he had to get away from what he had done with his entire life, and from the shadows of this terrible night.

At first, he had been heedless of the thirty-below temperature and the zero visibility. His thoughts were wholly occupied with the scene which had occurred between himself and the woman in the restaurant. She had pulled a gun on him! On *him*! What had happened would not have happened if that insane bitch had not threatened him...

"Leave!" she had ordered, but Cassell had shaken his head. He was not refusing, but confused as to what this foolish woman was so upset about.

"You don't understand," he had said, exhaling a gin-laden sigh.

"Oh, yes, I do understand. You get out of here and leave that poor child alone! I'll kill you if I have to, you bastard!"

Cassell had stared with incomplete comprehension at the gun. He had seen the woman's finger beginning to squeeze the trigger. He had made an awkward grab which unbalanced him. He had fallen forward, his hand pushing the gun back against the woman's chest.

The gun had fired. The woman flopped back into her chair. Her free hand swept a packet of letters to the floor. The gun clattered beside it. There had been complete silence for a long minute, followed by a sad, quiet thump as one of her shoes came free of her foot.

Cassell had ended on his knees, his hand on the small silver gun. He had picked it up and stared at it, sniffing at the sudden scent of brimstone, dropped it again. Then he had heard a thumping of feet on stairs from somewhere close by in the building, and panic replaced his shock. Cassell had scrambled to his feet, and, disoriented, run with clumsy haste to the nearest door, which led into the kitchen, then through another door, marked EXIT. In a moment he had been loping awkwardly through the arctic chaos.

At times as he ran he was hip-deep in snow; at other times he was on ground that had been stripped to the grass by the wind. The barren patches were solid ice and even more treacherous than the drifts. At one moment he floundered through great white masses, and at the next he slipped, stumbled, and fell heavily to the bare ground. Wherever he ran, he made no progress, nor did he have the least notion of what progress might be.

Something came roaring at him out of the white miasma. Cassell saw a gleaming shape which spat flame and accusation as it rushed toward him. It screamed as it passed, and Cassell felt its hot breath on his cold skin.

The roaring faded, and Cassell knelt in the snow, panting, exhausted. In the wake of the beast came Cassell's women and his girls, the females he had loved or hated in his lust. He struggled back to his feet, and tried to run from them. Even more tenaciously than the storm, they clung to him, plucking his ears, his nose, nibbling at his extremities, tweaking his frostbitten cheeks, snatching and tearing his hair. Like the Fates they attacked him, like the harpies of the ancient south and the witches of the ancient north, like the banshees and the vengeful female sprites of every nether world. The torments they devised for him were worse than any winter could dream or execute.

From time to time, he thought he could see, through the gusts, the gargantuan face of the dead woman, shouting commands like Hippolyta to her Amazon army; her visage rode the wind with its eyes shut, as if in sleep, but the lips were open and in motion, and Cassell heard words in echoing ululation: "Monster... monster!" the voice accused.

"It wasn't my fault!" Cassell screamed hoarsely up at the demon-thick sky. "You threatened me! I had to defend myself..."

Claws and fangs tore at him, but the soft parts savaged him more excruciatingly than all the rest. Breasts scalded him; bellies seared him; loins, smelling as rich and gynaceous as they might in the heat of a lubricious embrace, oozed vitriol, lava, and plague.

The snow women's numbers grew as he raged blindly through the blizzard, and his panic grew apace, until it seemed that he was adrift in a frigid sea of furious femininity, wherein every wave had a score to settle and a rite of vengeance to celebrate.

The hellish host of spirits was merciless. They allowed no repentance and gave no quarter. They were deaf to his bellowing, and to his whining as well. Even his sobs, when finally he ceased to struggle and fell full-length in the snow, left them unmoved, unforgiving, cold and unrelenting as the dreadful night itself.

38.

For the unhappy group at the Blue Bayou, the hours until dawn passed without further event. Some managed a few fitful patches of sleep; some talked, especially the newly garrulous Oswald; others discussed the murder, but with no new insights. Joe told a story or two, played a few songs. As the night wound to a close, so did the storm. By the time the sky began to brighten, only a few scattered flurries remained, like random feathers left over from a province-wide pillow fight.

The telephone lines were repaired, and Keyes was at last able to get through to the local authorities. He gave a summary of the death of Belle Feist. The police, followed by an ambulance, arrived in the wake of the first snow plow along the highway.

It was late afternoon by the time the police cruisers returned everyone to the Blue Bayou (except for Oswald, who had been admitted to Stratford General Hospital for observation) to pick up their vehicles and disperse along their separate ways.

It had been a noisy and confusing several hours at police headquarters in downtown Stratford, during which addresses, fingerprints, and statements were taken. An officer had politely returned Keyes' cassette recorder to him, and with a smile said that the forty minutes of country-and-western music would be of little use to the investigation; only Hawkwind's monologue had survived— the biker had obviously noticed that the infernal machine had been set to tape directly from its self-contained radio, and had reset it. Hawkwind had then recorded a mouth-watering and mind-altering recipe for chocolate-hashish brownies which would have been the envy of Alice B. Toklas; the youth's voice on the tape swore by Zoroaster that the secret had been handed down to him by his own mother.

Everyone was told to remain in the city for a couple of days. While Keyes was climbing out of the cruiser back at the Bayou, he overheard a brawny young sergeant inquire as to Louise's availability for a social outing at some later date. Keyes did not, however, overhear her response.

"I had to call the CAA," George Cook complained with his usual grating volume. "We'll never get the car out of that drift without help."

"I'd be glad to help out," Keyes said, "but my little Toyota doesn't have much power..."

"Toyota!" George snarled derisively, being that kind of Canadian who hates all foreign-made machines, except those made in the USA.

"We'd give you a hand," said Gordy Doig, "but our insurance doesn't cover it, so it's against regulations."

"I'd help," Louise said, "except that I'm not allowed to. Bus drivers—"

George cut her off, not really surprised, since he had rarely helped anyone in his life. "Never mind. The CAA should be here soon."

"So, who needs a lift into town?" Louise called in her big voice, as if there might be others lurking somewhere about the premises who required transportation.

"I do," Joe said. "Can you drop me at the Wabash-Canon Bar & Grill?"

"Sure thing. I might even pop by there tonight and catch your act."

Joe beamed. "You do that— I'll sing a song for you."

"Don't put yourself out." Louise turned to Jennet. "Come

on, kid. You're going to stay with me till this business gets sorted out." Jennet looked doubtful, but Louise was not so easily put off. "You said you didn't think you could handle going back to Cornerpost right away— where else do you have to go? You'll like it: top floor of a great old house, view of the river... VCR and stereo, and I'm on the road a lot, so you can just laze around and chill out. Maybe figure out what you're going to do."

Jennet almost smiled, but looked uncertainly at Keyes and Corinna.

"Why not?" Keyes said. "You need a place to crash for a while. I'd let you bunk in my house, but the neighbours might turn me in as some sort of pervert."

"You *are* some sort of pervert," Corinna informed him, "but luckily you're of an extremely rare and mostly harmless sub-species. Listen, Jennet, here's my card with my home number in Toronto on it— you need anything at all, you call me."

"How about that?" Louise said. "Almost an entire family!"

Jennet did smile then. "Thanks..."

"Let's hit the trail!" Louise boomed.

"Hasta la vista, amigos!" Joe McKendricks called over his shoulder as he boarded the bus.

The roadkill patrol left, too, with Gordy looking smug and Peavine looking tremendously hung over. The CAA tow truck arrived as the Ministry truck was pulling out, so even the Cooks and the Bakers were able to depart. Darlene and Earlene walked hand in hand, and turned to wave with a certain amount of friendliness; their husbands did not.

"I reached my friend Betty Beardsley," Keyes said as he and Corinna walked to the Tercel. Marcia Delaney had not been in her office, and Betty had heard nothing. "My house deal hasn't closed—" Keyes shuddered privately" —so she booked me in at

The Jester's Bells for the night— I had her get you a suite, too. What say we get some dinner before we hit the Wabash?"

"No argument here! Can you get this little beast started up again?"

"Of course I can," Keyes pronounced with a certainty that he did not altogether feel. But the rust-afflicted Toyota's engine turned over cheerily, as if it led a charmed life; which, Keyes was convinced, it did, as do the most unlikely people and things in this existence. Perhaps even driveways. He hoped.

39.

"Slow down, Gordy," Peavine muttered when they had driven a couple of miles. This was the first he had spoken in many hours.

"I'm not going very fast!"

"I know, but there's something on the road up ahead... there— pull over."

Gordy squinted through the windshield. It was a fine day, and the cairns and domes and rough pyramids of accumulated snow shone and flashed in the brilliant sunlight like some new civilization born out of the cold chaos of Ragnarok.

"I don't see anything," Gordy said with more stubbornness than he might have openly exhibited the day before.

"Pull over!"

Gordy was no longer so much in awe nor so terrified of his partner as he used to be, but he decided not to argue with this particular tone of voice. He pulled over. Just ahead of them, in the deeply drifted ditch, an arm reached grotesquely toward the sun. It was stiff as the rails in the fence beside it. The fingers, blackened by frostbite, clutched at or pushed away something that wasn't there, and perhaps never had been.

Peavine descended from the cab of the truck, got a shovel from the back, and trudged toward the arm. In a few minutes, he had uncovered the frozen corpse of Burgess Cassell. Then he returned to the truck.

"Dead man," he reported laconically to Gordy.

"Geez! What should we do with him...?"

"Whaddaya think?" Peavine snarled, his old self again. "Get out one of the *big* bags, and take him in."

Gordy trembled, but nodded, and soon the two men were moving about slowly in the radiant day, attending to their work.

40.

During their spaghetti dinner at Surly's, a restaurant on Wellington Street in Stratford's downtown core, Keyes and Corinna briefly rehashed the events of the past twenty-four hours, but decided to put Belle's death out of their minds for the night at the Wabash. Keyes had called Marcia Delaney the first chance he'd had; she was still not in her office, so he'd left a message with her secretary about where he would be, and crossed his fingers. Then he had notified those few residents of Stratford who might care that he was safely in town. He had also called his mother in Montreal, to invite her to visit him in a month or so, as soon as he was settled in Stratford. He admitted to himself that his optimism was reckless, since he had no idea how Marcia had fared in her negotiations.

All things considered, Keyes and Corinna arrived at the Wabash-Canon Bar & Grill in fair humour, having eaten well and groomed themselves and their clothing.

The Wabash had been a livery stable in Stratford's youth, then a warehouse, was once almost a parking lot, and now was a popular country and western venue. Although Stratford is as far from the Wild West as The Rhinestone Cowperson, Keyes could not help feeling that the Wabash was closer to the real thing than that glittering, charming, ultimately bizarre Toronto establishment.

The majority of the sizeable crowd at the Wabash was working class, if not working poor. Most of the flannel shirts were faded from the sun and had not been purchased in that condition as vintage clothing; most of the boots were worn and cracked from hard usage; and most of the patrons were decidedly heterosexual. Keyes admired a fashion among the ladies of high Western boots and short denim skirts.

The music was loud and aggressive, the customers louder, and the dancing was vigorous. About twenty minutes after they had joined Moanin' Joe at a table where he was tuning Ivy near the empty stage, oblivious to the din around them, Keyes heard a deliberately mangled version of his name from the direction of the entrance.

"Jon-Clod!" Like a fanfare, the massive baritone voice of Seamus O'Reilly— the subject of Keyes' last biography— blared across the tumultuous dance floor, "Cousin!"

Keyes stood up and beamed through the pall of cigarette smoke. He waved at his old friend, who, mindless of the figure of the dance in progress, veered in Keyes' direction. Dancers veered in their turn to avoid being run down. Several couples parted and reformed in Seamus' wake. Angry looks and surly comments were tossed after him, but none of these worried the big actor. He moved, indeed he lived, like one of nature's major forces.

Keyes pulled out a chair for Seamus. Before the actor sat down, however, he asked to be introduced.

"Do I know these people?" he said. McKendricks was included in the term "these people," but Seamus had eyes only for Corinna.

"My friend Corinna..." Keyes began, meaning to go on to this friend's other name.

Before he could, Seamus raised his Olympian head and declaimed:

Corinna, pride of Drury Lane,
For whom no shepherd sighs in vain–

"I beg your pardon!" Corinna snapped, unsure whether or not to be amused.

"Swift... not a nice poet, actually." Seamus turned abruptly to the tall cowboy. "My name's O'Reilly."

Joe held out his hand. Seamus took it briefly, then sat down. Keyes watched to see how they would get on, these two men he liked so much. It was easy for him to imagine they would not get on at all, the Shakespearean actor and the honky tonk singer. There was no sign of tension between them, however, no bristling or baring of fangs.

"What are we drinking?" Seamus asked, all amiability. His attention soon returned to Corinna. "An editor, Jon-Clod tells me. Fascinating."

Corinna had always thought herself fascinating and was immediately interested in anyone who found her so, especially if that someone was male. Soon she and Seamus had their heads together, while she told him about her life and work. O'Reilly played fascination with consummate skill. He was the bird, and Corinna the elegant cobra.

Keyes and McKendricks returned to a game they had been playing, although it was unacknowledged as such: Keyes was exercising a bad habit common to biographers and archaeologists—unearthing the secrets of the past, regardless of what ancient spirits might thus be disturbed. For his part, Joe was exercising the basic right of the wandering bard, muddying the informational waters at every opportunity. Both men were enjoying themselves.

The entrance of another of Keyes' acquaintances, Betty Beardsley, was unavoidably less arresting than O'Reilly's had been, although her tall gauntness and punk-cut white hair did garner her a share of stares and comments. She appeared at Keyes' shoulder, slipped into a chair beside him, and gave him a brisk kiss.

"You look tired," she said, her pronouncement more military than motherly.

"I didn't get much sleep last night," Keyes explained. "How's my house?" Although Betty had been initially responsible for Keyes' purchase of this particular residence, he had not yet told her about the complications. The cottage's former owners were Betty's younger brother, Bobby, and his wife, who were relocating to Australia.

"Surviving. The painters cleared out an hour ago. I've got your keys here somewhere. Bobby whined about handing them over before the papers were signed... all sorts of bullshit about insurance and liabilities. I don't know how a Tory like him ended up in our family! I finally had to threaten him with making his colourful personal habits public." Betty rummaged through a leather backpack large enough to hold a goalie's equipment, and went on rummaging as she spoke. "Galantine, I'm afraid, has some personal problems..."

"And who would Galantine be?" Keyes asked politely, expecting to be told of the traumas of one of Betty's actor guests at the Bed and Breakfast she operated.

"Your cat."

"My *what?*"

Betty was unfazed by his obvious shock at being in sudden possession of a pet.

"She was Bobby and Audrey's cat. Now she's a housewarming present from me. You're going to love her, Claude, as soon as she gets over her present mood: pissed off." Betty found the house keys and passed them over to her friend. "You need to get another set."

"Right. How can you tell?"

"Tell what?"

"That Galantine is pissed off."

"She's been killing mice—"

"Isn't that what she's supposed to do?"

"— and eating them in your bed. She never eats the entire mouse, unfortunately."

"Terrific!" Keyes groaned.

"It's not her fault. I suspect she was traumatized as a kitten, and we humans have a responsibility to our animal companions."

"I have to work..."

Betty glanced across Keyes at Corinna, for whom she had little love.

"I can see where some aspects of what you do might be made to seem like work," she said sourly. "Galantine did a bird, too."

Keyes groaned. "In my bed?"

"A purple grackle, I believe. Hard to tell, but the plumage suggests..."

"Plumage? In my bed?"

"She seems to consider the mattress her own private killing ground. I cleaned it up as best I could."

"You're a pal, Betty."

Betty scowled a comic scowl, then turned on a bright look of camaraderie toward the others. "I don't think I know all these people."

Keyes introduced Betty to his new friends. "Moanin' Joe is on the bill tonight."

Betty looked at the cowboy. "You're a singer?"

"There are several schools of thought about that," Joe said, grinning. "I know lots of songs, though, and I play pretty good guitar."

Louise and Jennet showed up next. Both went immediately to Joe and gave him hugs. Keyes saw that Jennet, too, looked tired, but there was an aura of quiet peace about her, like a Renaissance Madonna.

"We haven't missed anything, have we?" Louise asked. "You haven't started yet?"

Joe shook his head. "Have to wait until all these dancers slow down. I don't sing while they're two-stepping, only between sets, when they're drinking." To Jennet, he said, "Speaking of boozing, I had a word with the manager, and he said as long as you're not drinking alcohol he'll overlook your age this once— but not to start hanging out here or anything."

Jennet took a quick look around. "Unlikely to be a problem," she said.

Again Keyes made introductions. Seamus rose to his feet melodramatically.

"Mademoiselle," he intoned gallantly to Jennet, and to Louise: "Madame!"

Louise made a face. "Not any more I'm not."

"Mademoiselle, then." Seamus was clearly impressed by Louise. He was easily impressed by women, not by all of them, but by most.

"Is he always like this?" Corinna whispered to Keyes.

"I couldn't say always, but he is whenever I've been with him. Are you always like this, Seamus?"

"Like what?"

"Never mind. You're not in rehearsal yet, are you?"

"Soon." The word, simple as it was, rang portentously from O'Reilly's chest.

"Do I know what you're playing?"

"Probably not. There's been a certain confusion at HQ. I'm not doing anything I haven't done before except the priest in *T'is Pity She's a Whore*."

"Are they doing Ford at last?" Keyes said with real delight. "It's a grand piece."

"And it plays like gangbusters. I've only seen it once, and that time in French. Visconti did it in Paris years ago. The priest isn't a big part, but he does deliver the greatest hellfire and brimstone sermon in the English theatre. I expect to be tremendous."

"And I expect nothing less. But why don't people do the play more often? The title, I suppose."

"That and the fact that incest isn't a very attractive subject for our puritanical times."

Keyes shrugged. "Not in plays, maybe, but the talk shows are full of it, and so are the newspapers."

"Yes, even in sleepy Perth County. Nevertheless..." Seamus rose to his feet. His mass cast a heavy shadow over the table.

"Where's the tapster?" he bellowed. "Where's the barmaid? I want a drink, and somewhere back there, a drink wants *me*."

Seamus strode away, moving in one of his "character" walks. The character this evening seemed to be Othello just back from Cyprus, someone magnificently martial in any case.

Showing disapproval of Seamus in her face, Corinna turned back to Joe.

"What are you playing tonight, Joe?" she asked sweetly, with a display of not very real interest, although Keyes appreciated the fact that she had made an effort to be civil, even friendly to Joe.

The cowboy pushed his hat back and scratched his forehead thoughtfully. "I was just thinking about that."

"You mean you don't know?" Corinna was genuinely surprised. She always planned *her* performances well in advance.

"Well, I know... sort of. It's a matter of getting started. Once I'm up and running the songs take over. One thing leads to another..."

"Don't you ever get stuck?"

"Stuck? You mean do I get stuck for a song to sing? No, I never get stuck that way. I know too many of them, and one thing leads to another."

"As you said." Corinna, in editorial mode, gently pointed out his redundancy.

"Right. Anyway, I've played in Stratford before, and even if I did get stuck, it wouldn't be any big disaster— the folks around here are pretty forgiving... Say, did you ever hear about the French couple who came here to go to the Stratford Festival?"

"No," Corinna said.

Keyes took a deep breath, suspecting some sort of hoax, or worse, the approach of a Joe-story.

"Well, there was this French couple, you see. Came all the way from France to see some Shakespeare..."

"Not Gilbert and Sullivan?" Keyes asked.

"No. Listen to what I'm telling you. This is a true story."

Keyes covered his face with his hands and groaned. Beside him, Betty nudged her elbow into his ribs. She had known several storytellers of Joe's ilk throughout her life, and had identified him as such very quickly; she was quietly enjoying the situation. Louise and Jennet weren't listening to Joe at all. In fact, they hardly seemed to belong to the table. They had turned away and had their heads together. They spoke in hushed whispers, and their conversation was intense.

"Don't mind Claude, Joe," Corinna said. "I'm listening."

"Well," Joe continued, "they pull into Stratford in the morning, and since they've got tickets to an evening performance they decide to spend the day seeing the town. They prowl around for a while, go into a restaurant for lunch. The Frenchman doesn't like the look of the place from the get-go, but then Frenchmen rarely do. He orders lunch and some wine. The waiter's a kid working his way through college or something, not really a waiter at all."

"Not a professional, you mean?" Corinna asked.

"Not even half, and he proves it when he tries to open the wine. He breaks the cork."

"That happens," Keyes said in defense of the non-waiter. He had once been a non-waiter himself.

"Yeah, well, he coaxes it and rassles with it, but only manages to bust the cork up worse. When he finally gets enough out to be able to pour some wine, the first glass is full of cork bits."

"Poor kid. So what did the Frenchman do?"

"He starts to demand a replacement bottle, but his wife figures that the kid'll have to pay for the bottle if they send it back... since he busted the cork, I mean, and also she's decided the kid is cute..."

"It's those little black vests they wear," Betty interjected, in the tone of one who knows whereof she speaks.

"Think so? Well, I wouldn't know, but the wife says she likes wine with cork in it, and to prove it she picks up the glass and guzzles the wine right down."

"Thereby destroying the evidence of the great corking crime, right?"

Joe nodded. "Now her husband is pissed off, so he tells her she can drink it all if she likes, and he asks for water for himself. She drinks the wine... every last drop, and can hardly walk when they leave the restaurant, which makes the husband more pissed off than ever."

"What a dipstick!" Corinna said. "What did he do then?"

"He marches her down to the river and loads her into a canoe."

"Did he think that would sober her up?" Keyes wanted to know.

"How would I know what he thought? I just know what he did. Puts her in a canoe and rows her out into the river. As it happens, this Frenchman isn't much of a sailor and doesn't know a thing about canoes. Can't even swim. He gets them out into the middle of the river, and while he's trying to turn round so they can come back, he tips the sucker over."

"That river's not very deep," Keyes suggested hopefully.

"Deep enough to drown in," Moanin' Joe pronounced with some authority.

"They drowned?"

"*He* did."

Joe didn't say anything for a moment, but Keyes knew that the story wasn't over.

"So the woman could swim?" Corinna said.

"Nope," said Joe, winking at Keyes from the side of his face which was averted from Corinna, "she couldn't swim a stroke, but she was so full of cork from the wine that she floated right down the Avon River until some kids fished her out— they gave her a little mouth-to-mouth and sent her back to France."

Keyes and Betty broke up laughing, not so much at the story itself as at the indignant glare on Corinna's face, which soon gave way to a smile. Then she began to laugh as heartily as her companions. Keyes was proud of her.

"Not bad, Joe," she said. "Not bad at all."

Joe bowed his head in acknowledgement of the compliment.

"The average human penis," Louise was saying, her voice easily audible in the hush that followed Joe's story, "is about six inches long..."

Jennet nodded wisely, as if she knew this statistic and much more on the subject.

"What on earth is she telling that kid?" Corinna demanded.

"Facts of life, I guess," Keyes said. "Birds and bees..."

"But a girl that age— a woman, really— she knows all that stuff."

"Sure, but she grew up without a real mother..."

"And Louise doesn't have children..."

"But the blue whale..." they heard Louise say before her voice sank again to a level appropriate to intimacy.

Whatever Louise was talking about, the conversation seemed to please Jennet. She stayed close to her new friend, sheltering in the lee of her, and listened with rapt attention.

Seamus O'Reilly, with beer in one hand and whiskey in the other, loomed again at the tableside.

"Veni, vidi, vici!" he boomed. He was having one of his Caesar moments, and, having successfully pulled focus toward himself, continued, "Strangest thing just happened to me at the bar. I was having a wee jest with the barmaid: when she asked me what would be my pleasure, I said, 'Hock, my good lady!' Then, with my most engaging twinkle of the eye, I added, 'Hic, haec, hoc, eh?'[8] expecting the lovely creature to back away in confusion from my sublime display of classical Roman. Instead, she continued polishing glasses, making no move to bring me my cup of wine. Finally, I demanded to know where my drink was. 'Why, sir, what about it?' this most excellent lady explained, 'You asked for it, but then you declined it!' Now isn't it encouraging to find such education in these rural surroundings?"

Both Keyes and Joe were gaping at O'Reilly with astonishment. Then O'Reilly began to guffaw.

"Angels and ministers of grace defend us! You didn't *believe* that, did you? It's *you* I'm having the jest with. Really, when was the last time you heard anyone speaking Latin in Stratford, especially in a charming though rustic tavern such as this?"

By common and unspoken consent, Joe and Keyes did not explain to O'Reilly the real reason for their reaction to his little

---

8. "This, this, this!"

joke. O'Reilly was so obviously enjoying their apparent gullibility that Keyes did not want to spoil his friend's fun.

Without warning there was a flurry of curly black hair and swirling scarlet skirts immediately to the left of Keyes.

"Claude!" Marcia Delaney shouted at aria volume into Keyes' ear. "It may not be Christmas, but I come bearing glad tidings which will bring you great joy— after you've signed these, you will own a house... complete with driveway." The lawyer pumped Keyes' hand furiously, while, with a flourish, setting a sheaf of papers on the table before him.

"What?" Keyes said, taken aback as always by Marcia's hyperkinetic presence. "You mean you did it?" Then Keyes saw everyone at the table staring at the two of them in confusion, and his manners overrode his excitement. He introduced Marcia, and then— without mentioning his possible Cosmodemonic solution— quickly summarized the disaster. This completed, Marcia launched into an explanation, with obvious glee.

"My learned colleague, Counsellor Weasel, had apparently been doing his legal reading through greed-coloured glasses. There was a misplaced decimal point in one paragraph of one document— right there, Claude, where it's circled. If he'd been paying attention to anything but visions of dollar signs, none of this would have happened. This twenty-two metres of disputed driveway was, if fact, *point*-two-two metres! You should have seen the looks on your new neighbours' faces, Claude! They were so embarrassed by the weasel and their own greed that they agreed right away to my suggestion that they sell you that little strip of asphalt that they do own... for one dollar!"

Marcia stopped, finally, to breathe, and Keyes breathed along with her, a long and expansive sigh of relief— he was saved from homelessness, from Mr. Cosmodemonic, and from Corinna's contempt.

Keyes' friends and acquaintances applauded loudly, and called out words of congratulation for him and admiration for his lawyer.

Then, as the accolades faded away, Moanin' Joe lifted his head. The recorded music had stopped. "That's my cue."

He stood up, uncoiling with a serpentine grace that only a few very tall men possess (Keyes was sadly aware that he, himself, did not; it had become painfully— literally painfully— obvious during his stage days). Joe adjusted his hat, pulling it low over his eyes.

"How's that?" he said to nobody in particular. Then, "Oh, nearly forgot..." He reached under the table and brought out a large square cardboard box. From it he took a hat; it was not quite a cowboy hat, being both wide- and snap-brimmed, more of a large fedora, reminiscent of the type of headgear worn by the Shadow rather than the Lone Ranger. It was pure white, with a shining hatband of black silk. "Here you go, J.C.— it'll keep the rain off and the wig warm; man needs a good hat."

Corinna took the hat from Joe's hand, and carefully crowned Keyes with it. It was a good fit, and Keyes turned his head slowly from side to side, so that his friends, both old and new, could give their judgement on his finery.

It was agreed by the company at Keyes' table that the hat was just right. Moanin' Joe grinned, then turned away and walked toward the low stage at the end of the dance floor.

Joe's performance was amazingly eclectic and of infinite variety; he exhibited a preference for Canadian songs, interspersed with those of his own composition, but did manage to include two or three Delta blues numbers, of which Keyes was fond. It was apparent that Joe was known by the audience, who shouted out requests with which Joe happily complied. He was joined onstage several times by local musicians, including an attractive, willowy accordion player whom O'Reilly tried to hit on by the evening's end, with much bluster but little success.

Closing time came all too soon, and Joe gave two encores. Keyes did not hear much of Joe's last song, as O'Reilly was trying to convince him of some complex Joycean theory that Prospero was Miranda's husband as well as her father, but the refrain of the tune stuck in Keyes' mind for days afterward, and he found himself singing it every once in a while:

He's no rocket scientist, that little guy Cupid,
I know Love ain't blind, but it sure is stupid.

And that, Keyes thought, is one of the most profound things I have ever heard.

Epilogue

It was three weeks before Keyes had reason to be at the Blue Bayou end of town again, this time on his way to Toronto for a meeting with Corinna to talk over his next book project, one for which he knew he would have to battle tooth and nail. He had decided that a profile of Moanin' Joe McKendricks was in order. According to some digging Keyes had done, the tall cowboy was well known in the alien world of Canada's country music performing circuit, and especially well known for a musician who had never recorded any of his material.

Keyes had rented a car for the trip, another Toyota, this one a startling scarlet which he was sure would infuriate his editor as much as the rusty orange had. He and Corinna had parted on ambiguous terms. The adventure at the Blue Bayou might have bonded them into lifelong friends, perhaps even lovers, if Corinna had a more sentimental nature. But, she was a pragmatist. The goings on at the Bayou had been all very well, but were not the reason she had left her city and braved the elements in deep southern Ontario. She had set out in search of a clown, and a clown she was determined to find.

The day after the Wabash festivities, Keyes had taken her in search of Jonquil, and they had found him, finally, not in Cornerpost but in West Dildo. The only problem was that the clown they found was only a Jonquil impersonator trying to cash in on the great man's reputation. He was also an appalling drunk, and the time they spent with him was anything but pleasant.

Keyes had sent Corinna back to the city on an evening train. She had thanked him for his efforts on her behalf, but was obviously frustrated and brooding. They had spoken on the telephone since, but only briefly, and Keyes wasn't at all sure how he stood with his attractive editor. In all their recent intimate time together, he hadn't managed to flirt with her in any convincing way, and he hadn't found her the clown of her dreams.

An unseasonable thaw had set in, and although there had been freezing rain in the morning, the clouds had since moved away. Cool sunlight shone on the slight, gentle greening of the land which never failed to surprise and please him.

The Blue Bayou was right where he had left it, but, like Belle Feist and Burgess Cassell, the motel had not survived the passions and storms which had drawn them together under its roof. The blue neon tubes were empty, the windows boarded up, and a FOR SALE sign formed an X in conjunction with the CLOSED notice.

Keyes pulled up in front of the building and shut off the car's engine. There was little traffic on the highway, and only a few bird sounds disturbed the comforting silence.

He stared for a long time at the windows, dark as Cassell's heart, empty as Belle's dead eyes; although Keyes still felt good about many aspects of his adventure— Jennet's escape from a sad and lost man, Oswald's return to normalcy— Belle was most often in Keyes' mind when he thought about the experience. Jennet was much happier now, and it was even possible that Cassell had found some sort of peace... but no one had saved Belle Feist.

A few days before, Louise De Wetering had left a long message on Keyes' new answering machine— displayed on its own special shelf in the den of his cottage— and the device had condescended to record her message intact and even to play it back. She had been told by a new friend on the police force that among the fingerprints on the pistol had been Burgess Cassell's, and it had been concluded to official satisfaction that he had murdered Belle, although his motive had not, and probably never would be, definitely established. As for Jennet, she was doing as well as could be expected; Barbara Cassell, although shocked, had been understanding and supportive of her stepdaughter's reluctance to return to Cornerpost, and so far continued to provide for her financially. Louise did not know what Jennet's plans were. Neither did Jennet.

Oswald, apparently, was in New York City at some prestigious institute for the study of neurological disorders. Louise believed, from the little she had been told, that Oswald might be serving as guinea pig, but a guinea pig in a very gilded cage. Keyes expected to turn on his television any day now and see a new movie-of-the-week, *Little Latin Drummer Boy: The Oswald Feist Story*.

For Keyes, there were days (the day Belle had been murdered, for instance) when it appeared as if each individual life was a separate language, rich and distinct... and almost completely incomprehensible unless one took the time to learn its most basic linguistic units. But most people of Keyes' acquaintance were too lazy to learn even the tongue of his or her own personal existence in all its complexities, let alone the phonemic and strophic secrets of the hundreds of other lives that crossed theirs during their however-many score and ten...

But Keyes had always found comfort in the fact that there were many elegant translation devices available to those who really wanted to understand the dialects of the human soul. Music and poetry were the two which Keyes favoured. Mastering such ethereal tools certainly required study and dedication, but there was an elaborate scholarly infrastructure that supported the quest for insight and enlightenment. And, even though the manuals of human knowledge— the poetry and operas and philosophies—

were frequently incomprehensible and contradictory, Keyes believed that such guides were still superior to floundering around alone in the metaphysical dark.

It was in the verse of William Butler Yeats that Keyes found words most relevant to the day of Belle's death: Things *do* fall apart, and the damned centre *does* refuse to hold. This time the rough beast had slouched toward Stratford to be born; or perhaps Keyes' old and trusted source of imagery, Wagner, was even more apropos to the particular circumstances— Ragnarok, the frozen end of the world, the death of gods and man alike.

As far as poetry was concerned, one thing was certain: T.S. Eliot was definitely *not* the ideal interpreter for recent events— April wasn't the cruellest month... February was, this year, anyway.

From time to time, Keyes could not help wondering if he could have done something, should have noticed something, that might have prevented Belle's murder. But, in his heart, he understood the bottom line of the human contract with existence in a dangerous and often uncaring world. No one man or woman, no matter how committed or resourceful, can protect all of the lost boys and running girls from harm.

But since when has that ever been an acceptable excuse for not trying?